The Deputy's New Family

Jenna Mindel

Recycling programs
for this product may
not exist in your area.

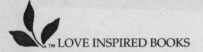

ISBN-13: 978-0-373-81789-4

THE DEPUTY'S NEW FAMILY

Copyright © 2014 by Jenna Mindel

www.Harlequin.com

Printed in U.S.A.

"I was hoping to talk to you about Corey," Beth said.

"Everything okay?" Nick asked.

"I'm not sure. Corey's afraid you'll send him back to his grandparents if he doesn't read well."

The woman didn't beat around the bush. "Where would he get that idea?"

Beth shrugged. "Your son told me in confidence, but I thought you should know because he's stressing about reading."

Nick nodded, but his gut felt like it'd been shredded. He'd left Corey behind before so it only stood to reason that his son didn't trust him not to do it again.

"You okay?" Beth's voice was soft.

His little guy had so much riding on those seven-year-old shoulders.

"I think Corey wanted you to come today because he's not easy around me anymore," Nick said. "He thinks I'll leave him. I don't know what to do about it."

"Maybe what you need is something fun to do together. Find some interests in common."

Right now, that interest was Beth Ryken. Corey liked her, and so did Nick.

Maybe too much.

Books by Jenna Mindel

Love Inspired

Mending Fences
Season of Dreams
Courting Hope
Season of Redemption
The Deputy's New Family

JENNA MINDEL

lives in northwest Michigan with her husband and their three dogs. She enjoys a career in banking that has spanned twenty-five years and several positions, but writing is her passion. A 2006 Romance Writers of America RITA® Award finalist, Jenna has answered her heart's call to write inspirational romances set near the Great Lakes.

But now the Lord who created you, O Israel, says:
Don't be afraid, for I have ransomed you;
I have called you by name; you are mine.
When you go through deep waters and great trouble,
I will be with you. When you go through rivers of
difficulty, you will not drown!
—*Isaiah* 43:1–2

To my sister, Lisa.

Although I was a pesky baby sister
who wouldn't stay out of your stuff,
you inspired me to love words—reading them (yours)
and then eventually writing them (mine).

You also taught me the real joy of haiku.
Thank you...for everything. I love you!

Acknowledgments

To Julie Mindel, Abby Carter and Tracey Miller:
Thank you for your rich examples and answers to
my many questions about reading levels, classroom
activities and standards. I applaud what you ladies
do! And I really appreciate your time as well as
giving me a glimpse into your worlds. Thank you!

To Kyle Sitzema: Thank you for your firearm
expertise. See, I finally wrote a red-headed hero!

To Christine Johnson: Thank you for sharing your
sailing knowledge. I couldn't have written that
exhausting scene without you!

Chapter One

ᐁ

"Miss Ryken, you've got a new student." The familiar voice of her school principal was warm but bore unwelcome news.

Beth Ryken didn't like surprises and a new student when the school year was two months from over wasn't good news at all. Core standard evaluations still had to be met and time at the end of the year was always fleeting.

Gathering her thoughts into a quick prayer for patience, Beth looked up but her gaze snagged on the tall man standing beside the principal. He was lean and mean looking in spite of the boyishness in his face. And he had short red hair. Not exactly a common combination. He also had an angular jaw and a strong nose that looked as if it might have been broken a time or two. Put him in a kilt and he'd be devastating to females everywhere.

Cool gray eyes assessed her. The man didn't

look pleased by her perusal. Annoyed, maybe. Cynical, definitely, but not at all happy.

Beth ignored those itchy fingers of attraction that scratched up her spine. Tossing her hair over her shoulder, she focused on the boy standing in front of the man. Red hair like his father and the same colored eyes, which looked lost instead of cold.

Beth melted. "Hello."

The boy gave her a hint of a smile aimed straight into her heart.

"This is Nick Grey and his son, Corey. They just moved to the area," her principal explained. "Beth Ryken is one of two second-grade teachers here."

"Welcome to LeNaro." Beth held out her hand to the youngster. "Corey, I have the perfect spot for you next to Thomas. His table could use one more boy to make it even. We're coloring tall ships right now and I'll have Gracie get an extra page for you."

Corey looked up at his father for direction.

He gave his approval with a quick nod while he released the hold he had on his son's shoulders.

Nick Grey did not wear a wedding ring. There wasn't an indentation or even a white mark left behind by a ring. If he'd been married, it must have been a long time ago. The only jewelry the man wore was a bulky watch clamped on to his wrist.

Typically, when dads dropped off their kids at a new school, it was safe to assume they were single, but something in Corey's eyes hinted at sadness. Was there a custody battle going on?

"Everyone, I'd like you to say hello to Corey Grey. He's new to our school."

The kids mumbled their hellos and then quieted when they spotted Corey's dad. Her students stared openly with awe, too. Mr. Grey's hair wasn't *that* red, so it had to be something else about the man. Like maybe how his pushed-up shirtsleeves revealed arms that were taut and whipcord lean. He reminded her of a power line that shot deadly sparks when snapped. Yeah, the guy looked a little dangerous.

Corey slipped his hand into hers.

Beth gave it a quick squeeze and led the boy toward the table and Thomas. "No backpack?"

Corey shook his head.

Beth glanced at his father before giving Corey a friendly wink. There was still a black one in the lost and found in the school's office. He'd need something to carry his books and papers home. "We'll get you set up."

Once the boy had been seated and introduced to his tablemates, Beth turned her attention back to Nick Grey. Not hard to do. Something about the man invited long looks.

But Nick watched his son with steely concentration before resting his unsettling gaze upon her. "I'll be back to pick him up after school."

"Whoa, wait." Beth held up her hand. "A little more information would be good."

Nick cocked his head toward Tammy, her principal. "She can fill you in." Then one more glance at his son. "I have to leave for an appointment."

Not quite rude, but terse came to mind, and authoritative. Was he military? The only military base nearby was a Coast Guard air station in Traverse City twenty miles south. Long commute, but maybe he wanted his son in a small school setting.

Beth reached a hand out to Nick. He was a good few inches taller than her, a rarity since she hovered near the six-foot mark. "Okay, well, nice to meet you, Mr. Grey. I'm sure we'll talk more once your son settles in."

Nick looked at her offered hand a moment before accepting it. "Sounds good."

First Beth registered his strength and then the warmth of his skin as his hand gripped hers for a firm shake. But looking into the man's eyes was what made her breath hitch. He really looked at her, as if delving down deep to see who she was. Not that he could possibly know with only one look but Beth still shivered.

And then he gave her a nod, let go and left.

Beth blew out her breath with a whoosh. "What was that?"

Tammy laughed. "Odd man."

Odd didn't quite cover it. Beth's heart still raced. "So what's the deal here?"

Tammy shrugged and lowered her voice. "Pretty vague, really. Mr. Grey showed up early this morning with his son and his medical records and filled out the paperwork for admission. There's no Mrs. Grey—she died a year ago. The boy's maternal grandparents are listed as the second emergency contact."

Beth's heart twisted. Corey Grey lost his mom at a tender age. Yup, sad story. Poor kid. She watched as he quietly colored his paper. So far the boy kept to himself with little interaction with his tablemates. Even bubbly little Grace Cavanaugh couldn't pull Corey into conversation. Was he shy? Or something else?

Beth continued to stare. Corey wanted a crayon, but he waited for Thomas to put it down before reaching for it. "What about testing?"

"Let's see how he does over the next couple of weeks, and then we'll meet and discuss a plan of action with the school counselor."

Beth nodded. Tammy was an excellent principal with an elementary teaching background. LeNaro Elementary School prided itself on meeting its students' educational needs first and foremost. They didn't push kids through the lower grades if they weren't ready to move on. If extra attention didn't work, they often recommended a student be held back. Not a popular approach, but the bridge between first and second was a big one. Preparation for third grade with its state standards testing was bigger still.

Beth had a bad feeling about Corey Grey. Loss of his mother plus a tight-lipped father and a new school usually added up to trouble for a seven-year-old. She'd have to keep a close eye on the boy. It wouldn't be hard to do. The kid had already stolen her heart.

Still, Beth needed to review the previous school's assessments before making any assumptions, but her gut feelings usually turned out correct. In Corey's case, that wasn't a good thing. Her guess was Nick Grey wasn't the kind of man who'd take bad news about his son very well.

She rubbed her arms as if a cold breeze had blown into the room. Nick Grey might be a difficult parent to deal with, but she'd find a way to figure it out. She always did.

At the end of the school day, Nick climbed into the driver's seat as Corey buckled up in his booster seat in the back. "How was your first day?"

The kid shrugged.

Nick gripped the steering wheel a little tighter and tried a more specific question. "What about your teacher? Is she nice?"

"Yeah, she's nice." Corey stared straight ahead.

"Good." Nick was beginning to think maybe he'd been wrong in taking Corey from his grandparents.

He'd been wrong about so many things, but Nick believed a boy belonged with his father. Was it selfish to uproot Corey yet again, so soon after losing Susan? Or was all this the price of leaving his kid behind while he finished up a tough case?

Lord, help me out here, please.

Waiting in the line of cars belonging to parents picking up kids, Nick drummed his fingers along the base of the steering wheel. This sort of thing was all new to him, but he'd get used to it. After this morning's appointment with the county sheriff to complete paperwork before he officially started as a deputy, Nick had finished unpacking their belongings. He had purchased a small house complete with a picket fence situated on two pretty acres a couple miles north of town. It was a start. A new start. One he prayed he'd get right.

"Hey, there's Miss Ryken!" Corey had suddenly come to life and waved out the open window. "Beep the horn."

"I'm not beeping the horn."

No way did Nick want to invite her attention. She was everything he liked in a woman on the outside, but she looked a little bit like his dead wife. Only taller and fuller, which, he had to admit, he liked even better. Susan had been obsessed with losing weight when she didn't need to. She constantly fussed over food, measuring and counting calories.

"Come on, Dad."

"The line is moving." Too late—Beth Ryken noticed them and walked toward their idling car. Nick swallowed hard.

"Hi, Corey. Mr. Grey. How was your first day?" She leaned down near the open window on Corey's side and her blond hair fell forward in long waves.

Nick watched the two cars ahead of him creep and then stop. He wasn't going anywhere anytime soon. "He's pretty stiff-lipped about today."

Beth gave him an amused smile. "Like father, like son."

Corey glanced at him and Nick thought he might have seen a glimmer of pride in his son's eyes, but it came and went so fast, Nick couldn't be sure.

"It was fun," Corey finally said.

Beth's perfectly shaped eyebrows rose. "Fun is good. That means you'll come back tomorrow."

Corey nodded.

"Miss Ryken." Nick tried not to stare at her. "Do you know of any after-school programs or good caretakers in the area?"

Her brow furrowed as the cars in front of him started to move. "Why don't you pull around so we don't clog up the line?"

Nick nodded and nearly kicked himself for asking her instead of the principal, but he needed the information. Should have gotten the leads before he'd moved here, but he believed face-to-face was always better than over-the-phone conversations. He was a pretty good judge of character.

Most times.

He'd never been wise when it came to women, though. He fell too hard too fast.

He pulled out of line and parked and then got out. "Corey, stay in the car."

His son stayed put.

Beth jogged toward him. Tall and strong. Confident.

Nick clenched his jaw. She was a sight to be savored.

"Are you looking for a structured program for Corey?"

"I start work soon, and I don't want Corey home alone after school. Any recommendations?"

"I can send a list of care providers with Corey tomorrow. We have an art-and-crafts-focused program after school, but it's only on Thursdays. I'm one of the teachers who staff it."

Nick looked at his car. Corey hung on their every word as he looked out the window. "That sounds good. Sign him up."

"I'll send a release form for that, as well." Her attention was caught by something across the street and then she waved.

Nick turned to see who it was and spotted an older woman dressed for yard work. Raking that lawn was bound to be a challenge considering all the flowers and statues that littered the grass.

"My mother," she explained.

"So your folks live right there?"

Beth's deep blue eyes clouded over. "Just my mom and me. My dad died when I was fourteen."

"Sorry to hear that." Nick tucked the knowledge away. He'd patrol this area soon and he'd pay special attention to that house with two women alone.

"Thank you. I understand that you're widowed."

"Yeah." Nick narrowed his gaze. He knew the kind of offers that usually came after that information. He was in no place to get involved with anyone, let alone someone like Miss Ryken, whose sunny nature seemed too good to be real.

"That must be difficult for you both." Her expression was open and honest. Sweet, even.

"It can be." Nick braced for an invitation he might want but wouldn't accept. He hadn't missed the blatant interest in her eyes when she'd checked him out this morning.

"We have a really good school counselor." Beth fished in her mammoth-sized purse. "Here's her card. She meets with all the students, but it would be wise for you to make an appointment to talk with her right away."

Nick swallowed his surprise and nodded. "Thank you."

"You're welcome. Gotta run." She smiled brighter than sunshine and headed toward the back of his car. "See you tomorrow, Corcy."

"See you tomorrow." His son sounded eager.

Nick flipped the card for their school counselor/social worker into his wallet. He'd call the woman in the morning. This school stuff was all new to him. His wife had taken care of that. After Susan's death, Nick's mother had stepped in to finish out first grade and get the boy started with second grade until she got bogged down with his sister's issues.

The past six months, Susan's parents had kept Corey safe and sound with them while Nick finished a delicate undercover case that took him out of town most nights. He'd had few days off and they were erratic at best.

He watched Beth cross the street and slip inside the modest home where she lived while her mother made a feeble attempt to rake up dead leaves from last fall.

Nick needed to step up. He wanted to be the kind of father his boy deserved, only he wasn't exactly sure how. He slipped behind the wheel and looked at his son. "Hungry? There's a café in town or the mini-mart and then we have to hit the grocery store."

Corey wasn't listening. He watched where his second-grade teacher had gone like a hawk. "Is that where Miss Ryken lives?"

"It is."

Corey looked at him. "Why can't I go there after school?"

Nick coughed. Not exactly something he could ask his son's teacher and she certainly hadn't offered, but that sure would make things convenient. "You really like your new teacher."

Corey nodded, looking deadly serious. "She's kinda like Mom, on her good days."

"I know." Nick felt as if he'd been punched in the gut. Corey had noticed the resemblance, too.

How did he handle that one? Ignore it, as he'd tried to do with his wife? She'd had too many bad days, and some days Susan barely bothered to get out of bed. Nick and Corey had been a team then. A silent partnership of protection against Susan's mood swings.

Nick hoped Miss Ryken's blond hair and blue eyes were as far as the similarity to Susan went. Corey's teacher had a sunny demeanor as well as good looks, but the instant attraction that had sliced sharp through him made him nervous. He'd fallen hard before, before he saw the darkness that lay underneath Susan's cheerful facade.

If love was blind, then Nick had been deaf, too.

* * *

"Who was that you were talking to earlier?"

Beth picked through her mother's latest shopping bag on the kitchen table, sorting out things to keep and return. "Do you have the receipt for these?"

"In my purse."

"Mom, you really need to stop buying stuff you don't need."

"But they were on sale."

Beth rubbed her eyes. Everything on sale ended up in her mother's tiny house. "We've got to stick to your budget."

Her mother gave her that look of tried patience. They'd been over this before. Several times in fact. "You didn't answer my question."

"What question?"

"Who was that tall man you were talking to?" Keen interest sparkled from her mom's eyes. Her dishwater-blond hair was covered with a flamboyantly patterned silk scarf, another "on sale" purchase. Who did yard work wearing *Ann Taylor?*

Beth waved her hand in dismissal, but her heart skipped a few beats at the mere mention of Nick Grey. "Oh, he's the dad of a new student in my class."

"Married?"

Okay, so every one of her friends was either married or getting married and her mom hoped the same for her. At twenty-six, it wasn't as if Beth was beyond hope, but she'd always been the proverbial bridesmaid. In a couple weeks, she'd repeat that role for her best bud and ex-roomie, Eva Marsh. Beth didn't need a reminder of her very single status, nor did she need her mother ferreting out prospects. Not that Beth had much success on her own.

She let loose a sigh. "Mom…"

"Well, is he?"

"No. He's widowed."

Her mother's smile grew even wider. "Interesting."

Yeah, very. Who wouldn't be moved by a handsome widowed man and his adorable son? "Can I have that receipt?"

"You're awfully bossy since you moved back home." Her mother bustled for her purse and then handed over the offensive slip of paper totaling the merchandise from a department store in Traverse City.

"Just trying to keep you out of bankruptcy." Beth smiled sweetly. She'd moved home over Christmas after she'd gotten wind of her mother's dwindling bank account. Something had to be done.

"You've got a smart mouth just like your father, God rest his soul." Her mom stripped off her work gloves and washed her hands. "What do you want for dinner?"

Beth shrugged.

Her mother used to get in hot water with her father over spending habits, too. On a cop's salary, they could afford only so much and her mother had expensive tastes. But she'd never been this bad with her shopping sprees before, had she? Maybe now that Beth saved every penny, her mother's spending glared brighter.

Beth's dad used to say the key to happiness was being content with what you had. He used to tell Beth to do whatever she loved and be grateful to God for everything. God had given her a passion. It was teaching. Her dad's had been for police work. It got him killed.

"Beth?"

She shook off her thoughts. "What?"

"Dinner?" Her mom cocked her head. "My, my, that man really got to you, huh? What's his name, this father of your new student?"

Nick. Nicholas Grey. The name kind of rolled easily around in her brain. "What about the leftovers from last night? Let's eat those and I'll make a salad."

Her mother made a face. "I suppose."

Beth chuckled. She'd called a halt to throwing out food, too. Her mother was a wonderful cook who loved to create masterpieces in the kitchen, but she made too much and then left it in the fridge too long. Since moving in, Beth never had to worry about packing something good for lunch.

Beth got up to make that salad while her mom reheated the chicken carbonara from Sunday's dinner. Beth glanced at the woman who worried her. Ever since her mom's work hours had been severely cut back at the airport in Traverse City, her mom's handle on her finances had slipped. Even with Beth's rent payments for living here. The shopping trips increased. Was she bored? Or was something else going on?

Nick Grey's question about after-school daycare providers filtered through Beth's mind. Could watching Corey bring meaning back to her mother's daily routine? Something about that little boy's reserve made Beth think her mom's flamboyant style might be good for him. It didn't get any more convenient than walking across the street from school.

The fact that Beth would get to see more of Nick Grey when he picked up his son brought a heady flip in her belly. Followed by guilt. This couldn't be about exploring the immediate attraction she'd felt for Corey's dad. Although it might be a nice side benefit.

Beth stopped cutting a carrot and looked at her mom. "Would you be interested in watching a seven-year-old boy after school?"

"Is he a good kid?"

"I think so." Another gut feeling.

Her mom's gaze narrowed. "Who?"

"Corey Grey, my new student. His mom died a year ago, and he seems a little lost."

Her mom's face fell. "How awful for him."

"That's why I was talking with his father. He asked about after-school care providers. If you're interested, I can let him know. If not, no problem."

"Let me think about it." But her mother looked interested.

Her mom could use the extra money, but Beth knew that wouldn't be the reason if she agreed. A softy at heart, Mary Ryken would be all over a child in need.

When they were done with dinner and cleanup in the kitchen, Beth headed for her usual spot at the dining room table to grade papers. After that she'd walk to the LeNaro community pool for her daily swim. Ever since moving back home, Beth found that several laps in the pool not only helped her relax, but it helped fight the extra calories from her mom's cooking.

Beth was no skinny mini. She'd always been tall and full figured. She tried to whittle her hips with swimming, but her body refused to cooperate. Her mother said size fourteen was not fat but normal. Still, standing six foot in bare feet wasn't exactly common for a woman. Not too many men were knocking down her door for a date.

She sighed and got back to work but the memory

of looking up at Nick Grey invaded her concentration. He was certainly tall enough.

Later when Beth skipped down the stairs with her duffel bag ready for the pool, her mom stopped her with a raised hand.

"I think I will watch that boy after school. You can tell your Mr. Grey that I'll do it until school's out and then we'll see. What's he going to do for the summer?"

Beth shrugged. "I don't know, but I'm sure he'll figure something out. We've got a couple of months yet. I'll let him know tomorrow. Maybe we could do a trial run, you know, make sure you and Corey click."

Her mother nodded. "Yes, do that."

Beth hesitated to leave. "You're sure about this?"

Her face broke into a wide smile. "Very sure. Have a nice swim."

"Thanks."

Walking down the sidewalk, Beth didn't bother to enjoy the sight of spring flowers blooming along the way or the mild warm night air. Her mind whirled. Would Nick agree to Corey staying with her mom after school? It might be good for both of them. And Beth couldn't help feeling a shiver of excitement at the thought of seeing Nick Grey more often.

She'd have to be careful, though. It wasn't smart to get involved with a student's parent when there might be issues. Could get messy real quick.

Chapter Two

Nick made breakfast. The eggs were too hard and the bacon a little too crisp. He wasn't a whiz in the kitchen, but he knew enough to get by. Knowing how to get by was what made him good at undercover work. God's grace had kept him alive during his last assignment, which had taken him away from home most nights. But that line of work was over. For his son's sake, he couldn't take those risks anymore. So he'd kissed the adrenaline rush goodbye and transferred into a rural county sheriff's department. About time, too.

Nick would never understand why that same grace hadn't covered his wife when she'd wrapped her car around a tree. But then, Susan might have made her own decisions about that. It wasn't *that* rainy the night she'd wrecked. He'd never know for sure. He'd make sure Corey never knew, either. He'd rather his son remember his mom's good days.

He turned away from the stove to holler down the hall at his son, but the kid was already dressed and seated at the kitchen table.

Nick slipped a plate in front of his son.

Corey stared at it for a few seconds before digging in.

Susan's mom made picture-perfect eggs. Susan had, too. When things were good, they were great, but then she'd hit a dark stretch and nothing worked well. If only they'd dated longer before they married, if they'd waited to have Corey, maybe...

Maybe he would have known, but then again, maybe not. Her wild bouts had come well after Corey was born.

"You're ready early." Nick sat across from his son and sprinkled his eggs with hot sauce before digging in.

Corey nodded.

Nick racked his brain for something else to ask. Getting his kid to talk to him was worse than questioning a perp. They went nowhere fast. "I'll pick you up after school."

Again the boy nodded.

They ate the rest of their meal in silence.

Nick grappled with frustration. He had a lot of ground to make up for leaving his boy behind for the past six months. Pretty hard to make a seven-year-old understand that he was safer with grandparents who lived an hour north of the city.

Another reason to transfer. Nick wanted to sleep better. He'd never grown used to worrying about some thug finding out where he lived. That had been the sole reason he'd refused to buy a house despite Susan's prodding that she and Corey deserved better than their Grand Rapids apartment.

The quick drive to LeNaro Elementary School was a quiet one, but the closer they got, the more Corey came to life. He'd lean forward, look out his window and clutch the backpack given to him by his lovely teacher.

Nick parked and unbuckled his seat belt.

"I can walk in by myself."

Nick looked at his son, careful not to bruise that seven-year-old ego. "I know you can."

"Then why are you getting out?" Corey's eyes narrowed.

"I'm going to talk to the school counselor. You being new and all, it's probably a good idea, don't you think?"

Corey shrugged. "I dunno."

Nick didn't, either. Beth Ryken had suggested it and since she probably knew more about kids than him, he was taking her advice. He didn't start work for a few days yet, so now was as good a time as any to see what this school counselor was all about and let her know Corey's background. He only prayed they wouldn't label him as troubled like the last school.

Entering the elementary school, Nick was struck by the noise of kids banging their lockers shut and chattering as well as the smell of breakfast wafting from the cafeteria. Maybe Corey would have eaten better here? Once he started his morning shift, Corey probably would. The principal had informed him about the school's breakfast program for kids dropped off early.

He looked down at his son with a mop of red hair and scattering of light freckles. The kid was the spitting image of himself as a boy. Sad, too. Nick's parents had divorced the summer he had turned ten. As the oldest, Nick had always felt as if it was somehow his fault. His and his sister's for fighting, for not being quiet when his dad came home exhausted from his shift as a Grand Rapids city cop.

A sharp tug at his heart kept him walking alongside Corey instead of turning into the school office. Crazy maybe, but he didn't want to say goodbye to his son. If he had kept his boy out today, they could have spent more time together. Doing what, he didn't know. Nick hadn't spent enough time with Corey ever since Susan had died. He'd always regret that.

Nick let work come first too many times. Needing to get the bad guys never flew with Corey. Those big eyes of his son's saw through his excuse for what it was. An excuse.

Nick was scared of raising a little boy on his own.

"What are you doing?"

"Thought since I'm here, I might as well walk you to class."

"I'm not a baby."

"I know." Nick caught a glimpse of a flowered skirt attached to the pretty second-grade teacher standing in the doorway.

Beth Ryken gave them a sunny smile that nearly knocked him on his backside. The woman was that beautiful.

"Good morning, Corey and Mr. Grey."

He gave her a nod. "Miss Ryken."

"I got my backpack, see?" Corey stepped into class without a glance backward.

"That's good. I'm going to talk to your dad a minute."

Corey actually smiled at her. The woman had charmed his son, as well.

She stepped out of the doorway into the hall. "He's a great kid. A little serious."

Nick sighed. "It's been tough on him since his mom died."

Her blue eyes softened. "And on you, too, I imagine."

Not as it should have been. He'd stayed undercover and sloughed off his kid first to his mom, then to Susan's parents. Not fair to them, even though they'd welcomed Corey with open arms. He cleared his throat. "Yeah."

"I wanted to tell you that I might have found an option for Corey after school."

"Really? Where?"

She took a deep breath and smiled. "My mother."

"Across the street?"

"Yes. She could use the extra income. I think she'd be great with Corey, but you'll want to meet her and find that out for yourself."

Nick couldn't believe his ears. Corey had requested the same only yesterday. "And you'll be there."

She looked confused. "Ah, yeah, after I finish up my day here. But you'll have to talk nuts and bolts with my mom. Pickup times, that sort of thing. I can introduce you after school today if that works."

"That definitely works. I'll pick up Corey here and then walk over with you." It was nice to talk to a woman at eye level. Corey's teacher smelled like spring and new beginnings. *Like kissing in the rain.* Whoa. Not a place his mind should go.

"And your mom's name?"

"It's Mary Ryken. She works part-time at the Cherry Capital Airport in Traverse City." Beth Ryken sounded breathless.

Nick stepped back, away from the allure of the woman in front of him. Her mother needed the money, she'd said. With gas prices the way they were, her twenty-mile one-way commute would be expensive. "I look forward to meeting her, and then we'll see."

"Great." That sunny smile again.

Nick couldn't look away.

"I better get started with class." Her cheeks went rosy pink.

"Oh. Yeah." He extended his hand. "Hey, thanks for this."

"You're welcome." She accepted his handshake and her skin felt soft.

He didn't want to let go but had to before he made a fool of himself. "I'll see you later, then."

She nodded and slipped back into her classroom.

Nick walked down the hall and checked his watch. He'd see the school counselor and then head for the sheriff's department. He'd run a background check on Mary Ryken before making any decisions.

Beth checked the clock on the wall. Just a couple minutes until the bell would ring, ending the school day. She glanced at her students working on their homework for tomorrow—a short reading passage with questions next to it.

Beth spotted Corey with his head down and wandered over. "Everything okay?"

He shrugged and sniffed.

Beth's midsection tightened as she knelt down. "What's up, Corey?"

"I don't want to do this." His eyes were red, but so far no tears had leaked out.

The bell rang and kids clamored for their jackets and backpacks. Corey stayed put and stared at his work sheet; he hadn't answered any of the questions.

Beth directed the kids as they left, all while keeping a close eye on Corey, who looked devastated. She gathered his things from the cubby locker and dropped them on the seat next to him. Beth was about to sit down and have a chat with him when Nick Grey popped into the classroom.

"Hey, bud, why the long face?"

Corey quickly shoved the work sheet into his backpack and shrugged.

Nick looked at her for direction. For the meaning behind his son's sulk.

She smiled, but her mind churned. "If you both don't mind waiting a few minutes while I clean off my desk, we'll head over to my mom's."

Corey's head jerked up, his demeanor totally changed. "We're going to your house?"

"Yes. To meet my mother." That was all Beth would say, in case Nick chose another option for Corey's after-school care.

"Cool." Corey slipped into a navy windbreaker.

"Do you want us to wait in the car?" Nick's worried gaze lingered on his son.

"Oh, no. I'll only be a minute." Beth kept her voice upbeat, but her initial worries about Corey returned.

Why had he been upset over a short reading assignment? The subject matter had been harmless enough. Tall ships and their sails. She'd have to talk to his father about that.

By the time they crossed the street, Beth had decided on discretion when she talked to Nick Grey. This was only Corey's second day in her class. New school, new home, no friends yet—it all added up to stress. Her principal hadn't received Corey's transcripts from his old school yet, so she shouldn't jump to conclusions.

Beth opened the front door and sniffed. Her mom had been baking. Nice. She gestured for Nick and Corey to come in and then kicked off her shoes. "Mom? I'm home and I brought guests as promised."

Her mother came toward them and looked right at Corey. "You must be hungry for a snack. I've got chocolate chip cookies straight from the oven."

Corey nodded and then looked at his dad.

"Thank you, Mrs. Ryken, that sounds wonderful." Nick held out his hand. "My name's Nick Grey and this is my boy, Corey."

Her mom gave her a quick wink. "Yes, Beth told me about you both. Come on into the kitchen."

The kitchen smelled like melted butter and chocolate, and Beth got busy pouring glasses of milk while her mom passed around a plate of warm cookies. Corey appeared to be on his best behavior. He took a napkin and carefully spread it on his lap before eating. That was definitely not a trick he'd learned from his father. Nick wolfed down a cookie with one bite while reaching for another.

Beth quietly slipped into a seat and grabbed a cookie, giving Corey a smile.

"I see you like flowers," Nick said. "There's quite a few in your yard."

Her mom nodded. "I love having them pop up willy-nilly every spring. They keep spreading and I love the surprise of where they'll go next. I won't mow my lawn until after they've bloomed. But my annuals are a little more organized."

That answer seemed to please him, and Beth nearly laughed. Nick was using her mother's erratic gardening as some sort of test, and evidently, she'd passed the first question.

"Beth, why don't you take Corey to fill up the birdfeeders while I talk to his father?" Her mom peeked at Nick over her designer-brand reading glasses. "If that's okay with you."

"It is." Nick smiled. It was an awkward smile, as if he wasn't used to doing it.

Beth let her gaze linger. Smiling was definitely something Nick should do more of.

Turning to the man's son, Beth slapped her hands on her lap. "What do you think, Corey? Do you mind going outside with me?"

The boy had finished his second cookie and had chocolate smeared in the corners of his mouth. He gave her a heart-stealing grin. "Okay."

Beth held out her hand to the boy. "Let's go. I'm going to need your help."

They stepped out of the kitchen onto the back deck. She knew they were in full view of Nick and her mom. A year before Beth's father died, he had installed big windows and a sliding glass door along the back wall of the kitchen as a Mother's Day present. Their backyard was large and her mother had birdfeeders scattered everywhere. Didn't matter where a person sat in the kitchen or living room, they'd have a clear view of birds scattering seeds.

Beth opened the door to the shed and grabbed a bucket. "So what happened today, Corey? Why don't you want to do the homework assignment?"

The boy shrugged. "I just don't."

She filled the bucket with birdseed and handed it to him. "Did you have homework at your old school?"

He shook his head.

"Did you get it done in school, then?"

He shrugged. "Grandma didn't give homework."

Beth frowned. "Tell me about your grandma."

"She used to read to me a lot and show me how to count."

"What about your teacher? Did she read to you, too? Or did she have you read the stories on your own?"

Corey stopped filling a low birdfeeder and looked at her as if she'd missed the obvious. "Grandma was my teacher."

"Oh." Beth closed her eyes. She definitely needed more information. She needed to talk to Nick.

Nick watched his son with Beth. He could tell that Corey talked to her. As they filled birdfeeders, Corey chatted easily.

He glanced at Beth's mom, who'd been watching him. She was a nice lady, if a little scattered. "I think Corey will do well here after school."

"I'd love to have him, and this works well with my weekday shift of seven till noon at the airport. Plenty of time for me to run errands and get home to meet Corey."

"Some weeks I'll have midweek days off and work the weekend. Would you mind Corey hanging out during the day on a weekend?"

Mary's brow furrowed. "What is it that you do?"

"I start with the sheriff's department in a few days."

Mary Ryken's eyebrow lifted, but the expression on her face had fallen into disappointment. "You're in law enforcement."

"Yes, ma'am. A deputy." Nick drained his glass of milk. Mary had offered him cookies until he'd stuffed himself.

"My husband worked for the same but was killed on duty."

"Yes, ma'am. I'm sorry for your loss." He'd looked it up. It was what made her a good choice. Mary understood a cop's life. She'd lived it. She'd understand if his shift ran late.

Her eyes grew stern. "Don't let it happen to you. That boy needs you."

Nick nodded. It was why he was here. Why he'd transferred out of undercover work. "I don't plan on it."

"No one ever plans on it, but it happens. And it happens to the best of them." Mary's tone hardened.

He waited for her to pass on watching Corey but she didn't say a word, only looked at him expectantly.

"The job's yours if you want it."

"I do." She smiled. "And weekends are no trouble. I'm a homebody on weekends, and Corey can go with me to church if that's okay with you. Our church has a good children's program."

"That would be great. We need to find one anyway." He wanted to get back in the habit of going when he wasn't working. It'd been a long time. A dry time.

Again Nick glanced out of the large windows. Beth and Corey had finished filling the birdfeeders and sat on a wooden swing together. Corey laughed at something Beth said. His son looked like what a seven-year-old should look like. Carefree.

Since he'd taken Corey back from his grandparents, the boy acted so careful, careful in what he did and said—if he said anything. Nick had learned to accept shrugs as their primary mode of communication. His boy had a lot to say to Miss Ryken.

Mary glanced at the clock.

Nick followed her gaze. It was closing in on four-thirty. Time to leave.

Mary smiled. "Why don't you and Corey stay for dinner?"

That surprised him, but then it didn't. If Mary Ryken cooked half as well as she baked, they were in for a real treat. He'd like to see how Corey responded to her. "Thank you, Mrs. Ryken. I appreciate your offer. We'll stay."

The woman stood. "Good, and please call me Mary."

"What can I do to help?" He also got to his feet.

"Not a thing." She waved him away and then stepped out of the sliding glass door. "Beth, why don't you show Nick around since Corey will be coming here after school. And, Corey, would you like to help me in the kitchen?"

Nick gave Mary a double take. She'd turned down his help.

As if sensing his confusion, Mary explained, "I might as well get to know the boy a little better, and you'll want to make sure everything is secure for him here. Beth will show you."

"Oh. Yeah, thanks." For a minute there, Nick thought she was throwing him and her daughter together.

Corey raced into the kitchen. "Really, I get to come here after school?"

Nick folded his arms. "That okay with you?"

His son nodded.

Nick remembered Corey's comment about Beth reminding him of his mom. Of Nick's wife. Was that why his son wanted to come here? To recapture a feeling of home and what he'd lost?

"Corey, why don't you wash your hands in the bathroom around the corner and then come back and I'll tell you what I need you to do." Mary had a nice way of issuing orders.

"Yes, ma'am." Corey had a nice way of following them, and he slipped out of sight.

Nick's sense of ease at this choice hit a speed bump when Beth walked into the kitchen. Seeing her regularly might be a problem. He couldn't muddy the waters of his life with an ill-timed relationship. Not when he needed to rebuild his relationship with Corey.

He sure could use a friend, though, and she was Corey's teacher. Keeping it friendly presented a unique challenge considering his track record. But it was only a couple of months until school was done. He'd figure out somewhere else for Corey to spend his days during the summer months because Mary worked in the mornings.

Surely he'd survive the next two months. They'd all survive.

Beth stood before him. "I'll give you the tour."

"We're staying for dinner." He watched her reaction closely.

"Mom always makes more than enough." She gave him another sunny smile.

"Do you mind?" They'd invaded her space.

"Not at all. Come on. We can chat about Corey."

Nick blanched at the serious teacher look on Beth Ryken's face. He got the feeling that she'd found something wrong with his boy and he was going to hear about it. "Lead the way."

It didn't take long to walk through the downstairs. Each room looked crowded with wall hangings and books and knickknacks. Beth's mom had collected a lot of stuff over the years, and that stuff seemed to pop up in odd spots like her flowers outside.

"There's a bathroom and two bedrooms upstairs. Just so you know, my father was in law enforcement and we have his firearms. But they're locked in a safe upstairs."

"No problem." Nick had guns at home, too, locked up where Corey couldn't get at them.

Someday he'd teach his son how to use and respect them. He'd start off with the BB gun his father had given Nick when he was Corey's age. Keeping that gun had been one of many disagreements between him and Susan. She didn't want their boy following in his father's footsteps.

Nick stepped outside with Beth. The day had grown warm enough to forego jackets. The backyard was surrounded by a tall wooden fence. Huge trees grew along the other side and their branches shaded part of the yard, lending more privacy.

One of Mary's more organized flower beds had been set up in the corner, complete with statues and greens poking up through the soil. The yard felt secluded, winsome even, as if he might find a secret passageway to some imaginary land, if a person was given to that kind of fancy. He wasn't.

He glanced at Beth. "You wanted to talk about Corey?"

She nodded and headed for the swing she'd occupied with his son earlier. "Maybe we should sit down."

He swallowed hard. "Okay...."

Whatever she had to say wasn't going to be good. It hadn't been good at Corey's previous school, either. The social worker there had said Corey displayed antisocial behavior. What was so antisocial about being quiet? Corey had been withdrawn, but Nick couldn't blame the kid. He'd lost his mom, and that school worried about how often he colored with a black crayon!

He waited for her to get comfortable before settling himself next to her, taking care to keep space between them. That pretty skirt she wore draped across her knees and swayed against her long legs, which were bare. Her feet were, too.

"What can you tell me about Corey's education?"

He gathered his wandering thoughts. "What do you want to know?"

"Corey said his grandmother was his teacher?"

Nick nodded. "For a little bit. Corey lived with his grandparents the last six months before we moved here. His grandmother pulled him out of school after Christmas break. She homeschooled him. Why?"

"Why wasn't he with you?" Beth's eyes widened as if she hadn't expected to ask that question. "I'm sorry, that's way too personal."

He felt his brow furrow. "No. It's okay. At the time, it seemed like the perfect solution. My wife's parents were glad to have him and I knew he'd be safe there. I was working a delicate undercover case that I couldn't walk away from."

"Undercover?" Beth's expression froze. She even scooted away from him a little.

There it was. That look of distaste for what he did was written all over Miss Ryken's face. Any interest she might have had in him died right then, he could tell. Probably a good thing, too.

"I worked as an undercover officer for years in Grand Rapids. I transferred into the sheriff's department here and start next week as one of their deputies."

"Oh."

Evidently, the Ryken women didn't like the idea of men in law enforcement. "I understand your father was a deputy sheriff, as well."

Beth stared at her hands. "Yes. Look, Mr. Grey, back to Corey. Can I ask why you allowed him to be pulled out of school?"

Nick leaned forward and rested his elbows on his knees. He'd been deep in finishing up his case and hadn't the time to double-check. Maybe he should have made the time. "My mother-in-law thought it might be best for Corey. I trusted her judgment and agreed."

"Did his grandmother follow a lesson plan, do you know?"

He should have known, but he didn't. Another failure. "Why? Is there a problem?"

"I'm not sure. Do you read together?"

Nick had plenty of excuses like working nights and leaving education concerns to his wife. He hadn't read to his boy since Corey started school. So many things he hadn't done for his own son. But that was changing, starting with this move north.

"No."

Beth gave him an encouraging smile. "I'll send him home with some books. Read together and see how it goes."

He narrowed his gaze. "What are you trying to say?"

"It's too soon to say anything other than I think your boy struggles with reading."

"Which means what?"

He watched her shutter her thoughts with a calm face. "We'll cross that bridge when we know more. After I hear from Corey's previous school."

That bridge was looming awfully close considering it was April. He knew for a fact that Corey's previous school had nothing good to report. It was why Nick had agreed to his in-laws pulling the boy out.

Nick looked into Beth's eyes expecting to find more disappointment, even censure, but it wasn't there. She was a blank page with that teacher face going.

At that moment Mary Ryken poked her head out of the sliding glass door to announce that dinner was ready.

"After you, Mr. Grey." Beth stood and waited for him to do the same.

His appetite was pretty much gone, leveled flat by Beth's concerns and the half-dozen cookies he'd ingested earlier. He'd make room, though.

As they walked away from the swing, Nick couldn't get the conversation out of his head. Corey had issues with reading. His boy had enough stress in his life—he didn't need more. As his father, Nick didn't want Corey to feel like a failure or be ashamed of his lack of skill with words. His kid was smart. He'd always been good with numbers.

Before they reached the door that would take them back inside, Nick stalled Beth with the touch of his hand to her arm. "Whatever I need to do to help Corey, let me know."

"Mr. Grey—"

He cut her off. "He can't be held back."

Her eyes widened.

Nick softened his tone. "This is important."

"Of course it is. All my students are important."

"That's not what I meant."

She held up her hand. "I know, Mr. Grey. We'll do everything we can."

"Thank you." But Nick had the sinking feeling that Corey's second-grade teacher had already written the boy off as a lost cause for this year. That didn't sit well. Nick had succeeded in getting some really bad guys off the streets, but at what cost?

Walking into the house, Nick was struck by the sound of his son chattering about baseball with Mary Ryken as they set the table.

"My mom's a die-hard Detroit Tigers fan," Beth said.

Nick nodded. Corey loved baseball. They used to watch games together on TV. One more thing they hadn't done in a long time. But all that would change, starting today with bringing his son to the Ryken house. He'd made a good move.

For Corey and maybe, with time, him, too.

Chapter Three

"Here, Corey, try this one." Beth handed him a beginning-level reader book about puppies.

Corey glanced at her and then cracked the cover. He stared at the page, muttered a couple of correctly read words and then pushed the book away. "I don't feel like reading."

She smiled at him, knowing this was the excuse he hid behind. "It'll get better with practice. I promise."

"Can I go across the street now?"

"Let's get through this book first."

The boy slumped lower in his chair.

"I know you can do it, Corey. And I'm here to help. Let's try again."

The boy let out a sigh and picked the book back up. Hearing the kid stumble over several words in a row, Beth's heart sank. Her suspicions had been correct. Corey Grey was nowhere near a second-grade reading level. "Let's sound this word out...."

It took a while to get through only a few pages. Beth was glad she'd called her mom before they'd even started and let her know that Corey was going to hang out with her after school. This was going to take patience, something she wasn't sure Corey's father had.

Nick Grey's reaction to Beth's concerns a few days ago still bothered her. He'd displayed such vehemence that his boy pass second grade. Was it a pride thing? Nick seemed to have more depth than that. She hoped he did.

Holding back a child to repeat a grade was openly debated within the LeNaro school district. Beth believed in some cases the hard choice was needed. Might even be needed here. But she wouldn't get Nick's cooperation, that was for sure. He wasn't offering up any information about Corey's old school, either. Beth called to rush those transcripts. The sooner she reviewed what was there, the sooner she'd figure out what to do. And find out why Nick had allowed his son to be pulled out.

She couldn't ignore Corey's failure to meet reading benchmarks, move him forward and hope for the best. The chances of him becoming more lost and falling further behind were too great. He excelled with math, proving the boy both was bright and could see. The need for glasses wasn't the issue here. So why did he lag so far behind in reading? What had he missed? And more important, could he catch up before the end of the school year?

By the time Beth and Corey finished the book and made their way to Beth's home across the street, Beth knew it'd take a lot of work to get Corey reading where he should. She had a theory, though. If she was correct, maybe they could go back and fix what Corey had missed.

"What took you two so long?" Beth's mom was decked out in a ruffled apron she'd purchased off a home-shopping show.

Beth smiled at Corey. "We were working."

Corey didn't look amused. Frustrated for sure.

Her mom clicked her tongue. "Corey, did you have anything to eat since lunch?"

"No."

"Well, dinner's almost ready. Go wash up and we'll eat right away. Your dad called. He'll be a little late."

Beth watched the boy do as her mother asked without hesitation, before she let loose her irritation. "This better not become a habit."

Her mom lifted her chin. "What are you talking about?"

"Corey's dad being late."

Her mother gave her a hard look. "That's between him and me. He promised to pay me extra when he's late."

Beth sighed. She couldn't really argue with that. Her father used to be late a lot, too. At least Nick had called.

"So why'd you keep Corey at school so long? The poor kid needs an afternoon snack."

Beth scrunched her nose. How much could she really share with her mom? "We were reading."

"He's behind, isn't he?"

Beth's eyes widened. "How'd you know?"

Her mom shrugged as her gaze shifted behind her before she focused back on Beth. "Set the table, would you? Corey, you can help."

The boy had returned. Reason enough for her mother's quick change of subject. But still, how'd she know? And if it was that easy for her mother to figure it out, why hadn't Nick? Or Corey's grandparents? Even worse, why hadn't someone done something to help the child?

Beth set the table, letting the dishes clunk hard as she laid them down.

Corey gave her a quick look with wide eyes. "Are you mad?"

That question stopped her cold. It wasn't exactly fear she read in his face but something close to it. Almost as if he'd braced for impact. It made her sick to ponder the implications of that single glance from a sad-eyed seven-year-old.

She wouldn't jump to conclusions. Not before reading those reports from Corey's previous school, if they ever got here.

Beth smiled, feeling like a heel. "No. I'm not mad. More irritated that I have to set the table, something I don't like to do, but I shouldn't take it out on the plates, huh?"

Corey surprised her with a big grin. The fear was gone, replaced by a sardonic expression that looked much too old for the child giving it. He looked so much like his dad. "They could break."

Beth grinned back. Had she read way too much into Corey's expression? "I suppose my mom wouldn't like it if I broke her dishes."

"No." Corey shook his head. "I don't think she would."

Beth watched him lay down forks and knives around each plate. He'd been through a lot at a young age, but were there additional concerns she should worry about?

A fierce sense of protection for Corey filled her. She'd find out, real quick. Starting with the boy's father.

Nick pulled into Mary Ryken's driveway. A few raindrops splashed against the windshield of his patrol car, promising more soon. He got out and rushed for the front porch and made it before the deluge.

Beth Ryken came out looking darker than the rain clouds overhead. "Can I talk to you a minute?"

That sounded like trouble. She looked stern. Still beautiful, though. Always beautiful. He took a deep breath. "Hey, sorry I'm late. I had to finish up the paperwork of an arrest."

"It's not that." A crease of worry marred her otherwise-perfect forehead. "Nothing serious?"

He let out a bark of laughter. "Maybe for the drunk and disorderly seventy-eight-year-old woman who refused to get out of the vehicle of the man who picked her up hitchhiking. The poor guy didn't dare touch her, so he called us. I thought the whole thing was pretty funny."

That didn't earn him any points. Beth's gaze grew cool. Icy. "Have you been using the books I sent home with Corey?"

He nodded. "Every night before bed we read one of those storybooks." Nick enjoyed revisiting that quiet time together.

"Who's doing the reading?" Her gaze narrowed.

"Both of us. Corey struggles, but I help him out." What was up with this woman? Two days ago she sent home the books. Why the grief when he followed her directions?

"They're barely first-grade level." Her voice had dropped to nearly a whisper.

The rain pounded the ground, but that was nothing compared to the bomb his son's teacher had thrown at him. "But I've seen him reading the backs of cereal boxes, and comic books."

"Probably following the pictures."

Nick stared at her with dread crawling up his spine. He didn't know what kinds of books kids read in what grades. Nick clenched his fists. Had she sent those books home to entrap him? To prove her point? That wasn't fair. Not fair to his son. To him.

At that moment Corey flew out the door. "Hi, Dad."

Nick looked at his boy. "Corey, can you wait in the car?"

His son glanced at Beth and then back at him. "Okay…."

"I'll only be a minute. Don't touch anything."

Corey's shoulders slumped and he flipped up the hood of his rain slicker and dashed for the vehicle.

Nick watched him get into the SUV cruiser and then focused on Beth. "There has to be something I can do."

"This late in the school year, I don't know. I'm sorry." Beth Ryken didn't beat around the bush, that was for sure.

"But there has to be something—"

The front screen door opened with a squeak, and Mary Ryken had a loaded plate wrapped in foil. Dinner? "We had more than enough."

Mary had made enough for both him and Corey to take home the previous night, too. "Thank you."

Nick's focus followed to where Beth pointed, toward the sheriff patrol vehicle. Corey was messing with something. "I've got to go." He stared hard at his son's teacher. "But this conversation is far from over."

He saw how Beth's eyes widened, but she didn't say another word as he ran for the car. His uniform got soaked in the process.

Nick slipped behind the wheel and set the foil-wrapped plate on the backseat. "I asked you not to touch anything."

Corey looked at him. "Are there games on this?"

Nick turned his computer monitor back around. "No. No games."

As Nick backed out of the Rykens' driveway, he glanced at the porch. Beth waved. Corey waved back. "What did you do at Mary's today?"

"I was at school with Miss Ryken."

"How come?"

Corey shrugged.

Nick drove with care, slow and sure. "Did she ask you to read?"

His boy's face fell. "Yeah."

"And you had trouble, huh? Like with the books we have."

More dejection. "Yeah."

Nick swallowed hard. "Corey, why didn't you tell

me you were having a hard time reading words? I could have helped."

"You weren't there."

The barb hit hard and true, piercing his heart with bitter regret. "Grandma and Grandpa would have helped you to read better."

Corey shrugged again.

It wasn't the kid's fault. Why hadn't Susan's parents picked up on it? Nick rubbed the bridge of his nose. They were dealing, too. He couldn't blame them. Maybe if he'd made Corey read more. If he'd been around…

"Dad?"

"What?"

"I think I made Miss Ryken mad."

Nick felt himself frown. "I'm sure you didn't, son."

"But she slammed the plates on the table. But not like Mom. Miss Ryken didn't break any."

Nick couldn't breathe. He never had the right words to explain Susan's odd behavior. Couldn't excuse it, either. They'd argued so much toward the end. Way too much.

"Don't worry. Miss Ryken wasn't mad at you." She was probably madder than a hornet at him, though, for letting his boy down. And rightly so.

Nick turned left onto the road that took them north of town to where they now lived. He needed to talk to Beth Ryken.

"Hey, bud, do you have recess before your lunch break or after?"

"After," Corey said. "Why?"

"Just wondered."

Nick knew his son ate lunch around noontime. So, maybe he'd stop by tomorrow. And see if he couldn't have a chat with Miss Ryken.

Beth checked her watch and growled. She was late. Way too late for her early-morning dentist appointment. She pushed down on the gas pedal and picked up speed. And then spotted the flashing lights.

"Really?" Beth slowed and pulled over to the side of the road.

Another growl escaped while she checked her glove box for registration and proof of insurance. Beth jumped at the quick tap to her driver's-side window. And then her stomach sank.

Deputy Officer Nick Grey with a shining gold star on his chest opened the door for her. He stood there tall and solemn. His mouth twisted into a crooked grin. "In a hurry this morning, Miss Ryken?"

Her stomach, which had dropped somewhere near her sandal-clad feet, now fluttered back to life. Why'd the man have to look so good in that brown uniform?

She let out a sigh. "Late for an appointment. I

guess I was going a little too fast, but there's no point now—I'll never make it in time."

"Do you know what the speed limit is on these roads?"

She squinted at him. Seriously? "My dad was a cop, remember? Fifty-five."

He cocked one eyebrow, but there was a definite twinkle in his eye. "I clocked you at sixty-eight. Not wise on back roads with deer roaming in the fields."

Irritation filled her. Irritation that she'd get a ticket, irritation that Nick Grey might be a low-down scoundrel who not only scared his little boy but didn't attend to his education. Even more irritating still was despite all that, Nick Grey grew more attractive every time she looked. "Just give me the ticket and we'll both be on our way."

"Would you step out of the car?"

Her eyes flew wide. "What! Why? I've got my papers right here. Look me up and you'll see I don't have a history of speeding tickets. This will be my first one."

His brows drew together and he looked stern. Downright scary, too. For a skinny guy, Nick was pretty intimidating. "I'm not giving you a ticket."

"Then why…?"

"I need to talk to you. Please?"

Oh, there was no denying that pleading look he gave her. And that only fueled the anger simmering inside. She got out of her car and slammed the door harder than she'd intended. "What do you want?"

"What's with the attitude?"

Beth didn't hold back. "I saw fear in your son's eyes last night and I'd like to know why."

Again the man only cocked one eyebrow, cool as can be. "When you slammed the plates on the table?"

Beth gasped and then sputtered, "I, uh—"

"Corey told me. Look, Miss Ryken, there's something you should probably know. My wife had mood swings. During one of her more manic ones, she smashed a stack of plates because I was late for dinner. Corey's a little sensitive."

Beth's mouth dropped open, and she slapped her hand over it. She was going to be sick. Corey wasn't afraid of his father; he'd been afraid of her!

"It's okay. No harm done. But it hasn't been easy for Corey, and I didn't make it any easier by sending him to live with his grandparents. But I'd run out of options."

Beth's heart broke all over again. "I'm so sorry."

"For what? Thinking ill of me? You should. I let my boy down."

"No, for scaring your son." Beth leaned against her car and stared at the cherry orchard across the street. She'd called that one all wrong.

The sun shone on dewdrops clinging to the tree buds, turning them into sparkling crystals. Those cherry buds would soon burst open into white blossoms. Just one of many breathtaking sights in Northern Michigan. She sidled a glance at Nick. Yup, breathtaking sights everywhere.

"It's okay, really. No harm done. His grandparents sugarcoated everything, afraid to raise their voices. I don't know, maybe they thought they were protecting him."

"Is that why you moved here? To get away from them?"

He shook his head. "I need to reconnect with my boy. His mom's issues forced us into a partnership, but then I left my partner behind and abandoned him."

"Living with his grandparents for a while is hardly abandonment," Beth pointed out.

"Tell that to a seven-year-old."

Beth gave him a sharp look. "I see what you mean."

He nodded and then leaned against her car, too. Right next to her. "You see why I won't let him repeat second grade? He's had so much taken out of his hands beyond his control. This will feel like one more failure for him. Another left behind."

It would feel that way to a seven-year-old. What a tough spot. Beth dropped her head back to look up at the clouds above. Her arm brushed against Nick's, connecting with what felt like a hard beam of steel.

She scooted away and faced him. "But it's so late in the year. I don't want him to get lost in the shuffle if he's moved ahead."

"It's never too late." Nick's voice was soft.

Beth drew in a sharp breath. Awareness hummed between them as he watched her. In his eyes she saw something stark and lonely and her heart responded. But she couldn't erase his worries and fix what had gone wrong in his life. He was off-limits.

She wasn't stupid. Beth knew mutual attraction when she saw it. When she felt it. There was no way she'd let herself get romantically involved with this man. Not when Beth knew how quickly his life could be snuffed out.

"I want to ask you a favor."

Beth tipped her head. Sounded like a big favor, too. "What's that?"

"Will you tutor Corey in reading?"

Beth stood straight and stepped away from her car. Away from him. He made her dizzy.

"I'll pay you, of course. Whatever it takes." He straightened, as well.

Beth whirled around. "I can't accept your money. I won't. He's my student. It's my job to help where I can...."

"But?"

She looked Nick in the eyes. So easy to do. "Repeating second grade might be the best thing for Corey. Have you considered that? He's new—it's not like there's peer pressure to deal with. Not yet. He could even go to the other second-grade class so I'm not his teacher."

"It's not the best thing. Not for Corey. And not for me."

Beth felt her spine stiffen. "That sounds like pride talking."

Nick laughed at her then. "Is that what you think?"

She folded her arms across her chest and stared down the deputy officer in front of her, knowing that wasn't it at all.

"Look, I can work with him all summer long, every single night, but I need a game plan. Something you're trained to give. All I'm asking is to get him where I can then pick up the slack come summer. Do whatever you need to do, only don't throw your hands up and recommend he be pushed back a year because there's only two months left of this one." Nick's steely gray eyes showed resolve.

Beth frowned and rubbed her forehead. Corey was already at her house in the evening. She'd have to get it cleared through her boss, but this was a special circumstance. What she did on her own time was her business. In the few days the boy had been with her and her mom, Beth had already come to love the kid. She didn't want to let him down, either.

She glanced at Nick.

"A big difference can be made in two months." He gently thumped his ticket pad in his hand. A reminder of the speeding ticket she rightfully deserved.

She laughed. "You know, extortion is illegal."

He gave her a slow grin that made her heart race. "Blackmail was never my intent."

Beth felt herself slipping, giving in. "You'll need to finish Corey's reading assignments after he leaves my mom's. And I'm going to hound you."

"I've had worse nightmares."

She imagined that was true. There was so much strength hidden inside that wiry, well-over-six-foot steel frame of his. And a lot of feelings were locked behind those gray eyes, too.

Beth held out her hand. "I'll do what I can. Have we got a deal, Mr. Grey?"

"I think we do, Miss Ryken. And we'll work hard on our end—I promise you that." He took her hand and held on, wrapping warmth and strength and all kinds of promises in one not-so-simple handshake.

Chapter Four

Come up with a plan. Nick had said that days ago and Beth had one. It had been slow coming together between progress reports for her other students and running it by her principal, but she'd done it. She'd even made up a progress booklet for Nick.

She riffled through the papers on her desk—Corey's papers from his previous school. Corey's old school reports were as confusing as they were disheartening. The transcripts showed a downward spiral that started before Corey's mom had died and then plummeted steeply afterward.

"Poor kid." Beth felt that undeniable pull for the boy.

Corey had been jostled between special reading groups, and he'd been labeled with emotional problems that were never clearly explained. Had no one seen through to the obvious? Corey didn't have a handle on phonics. Somewhere along the line, he'd missed the mark and by the time his mother had died, his emotional stresses had kicked in and his dwindling grasp on vowel sounds and rules had slipped. It was no wonder he got lost along the way. He'd never mastered how to identify the trail markers.

Well, Beth knew a few things about marking trails. She'd start with flash cards, games, work sheets, whatever it took to get Corey more familiar with identifying sounds. And she had a stack of books for Nick so he could continue working with Corey at home in the evenings and on his days off. If he spent half an hour every day reading with Corey, it'd make a difference.

Beth's mom even promised to help where she could. The only variable she couldn't predict was Corey's reaction. His willingness to learn was key.

She put away the sensitive papers, locked the drawer of her desk and then scooped up her stuff. Exiting her classroom, she spotted the other second-grade teacher, Julie, calling it a day, as well.

"So, Beth, are you up for sailing the Manitous again this year?" Julie's husband was a hotshot attorney with one sweet sailboat. Gerry was more than the average amateur sailor. Sailing with them had become a tradition and a fun way to celebrate the end of the school year and the start of summer.

"I sure am." Beth nodded. "Count me in, only please, no setups this year."

Julie frowned. "Oh, come on, he wasn't so bad."

Beth tipped her head. Julie and Gerry had arranged a blind date with a guy from Gerry's office. He was way too short and arrogant besides.

Julie smiled. "You bring someone, then."

Beth's mind immediately shifted to Nick, but that brown uniform he wore made her shake away any thoughts of sunset sailing with the handsome redhead. "We'll see."

When Beth made it across the street to her mom's house, she was armed with phonics lessons. Walking into the living room, she expected to find Corey in front of the TV. Instead he sat at the dining room table across from her mom. The two playing a game of Battleship.

"B-3." Corey's hair hung in his eyes.

Beth's fingers itched to brush the kid's bangs back, but she remained quiet and watched.

"Nope. Miss." Her mom wore an evil-looking grin. "My turn. F-8."

Corey's face crumpled into irritation. "Hit."

"I'm home."

Neither one acknowledged her. They were caught up in the game. And it was close. Each had only one ship left, and Beth's mom dove in for the kill on Corey's big destroyer. It made Beth smile as she slipped upstairs to change into jeans.

When she returned, Corey had put away the pieces while her mom started dinner. "Who won?"

The look of disgust on Corey's face clued her in.

"Sorry. She always beat me, too. Are you ready to play some different games?"

The boy looked cautious. "Like what?"

"Sound games." Beth spread out her flash cards.

"That's schoolwork, isn't it?"

Beth met the boy's wary eyes. "Did your dad tell you that he asked me to be your tutor?"

"Yeah."

"Did he say why?"

Corey looked down. "Because I don't read good."

Beth touched his hand and gave him a big smile. "You will, Corey. I promise, in time you will read much better."

He looked at her with a lot of doubt in his face, but she spotted hope shining in his eyes.

Thursdays after school, Beth helped staff a kids' art program. She milled between tables, helping where needed but mostly watching kids create. Corey sat at a table littered with paper, crayons and markers he hadn't touched.

Grace Cavanaugh worked beside him drawing a house on a piece of yellow construction paper. She cut out trees made of brown and green paper and then pasted them on the yellow. She glued cotton balls for clouds.

"Don't you like to color?" the little girl asked.

Corey shook his head.

"Why?"

He shrugged.

"This is our house. It's for my mom." Grace stuck the paper in Corey's face.

"My mom died." Corey flicked the edge of the paper away.

Beth sucked in a breath, but she remained quiet and watched the two kids interact.

Grace set her paper down and tipped her head. She considered what Corey had said for a few seconds and then shrugged her shoulders. "That's okay. I don't have a dad. Maybe you'll get a new mommy. Want me to help you get started? I know where everything's at."

Corey nodded.

"C'mere, then."

Beth's eyes stung when Corey followed Gracie to the paper bins. She directed him to pick a color and he did. And then he followed her back to the table while she rattled off a host of things he could draw and she promised to help. God bless little Gracie. She'd broken into Corey's shell.

"Hey, Beth, got a minute?" Diane, their school counselor, leaned against the door.

Beth scanned the room for the other teacher helping out. She spotted her assembling the supplies they'd need for tonight's lesson in painting.

The kids were busy chatting and hanging up their backpacks. She could duck out for a few. "Yeah, sure."

Diane nodded toward the hall.

Beth gave the other teacher a heads-up and then followed Diane out of the art room. "What's on your mind?"

"I understand you're tutoring one of your students. The new boy, Grey, is it?"

Beth folded her arms. "Corey Grey. I cleared it through Tammy. The boy's behind in reading."

"Where are you working with him?"

"My mom watches him after school, so we work at home. Why?"

Diane looked concerned. "I had a long talk with Mr. Grey about his boy still grieving. Corey might latch on to you as a maternal replacement, so it might be wise to stay in teacher mode."

Gracie's words whispered through Beth's mind. *Maybe you'll get a new mommy.* And something deep inside twisted, wishing...

Not going there. Beth cleared her mind with a firm nod. "Gotcha."

"We should compare notes in a week or so to see how he's settling in. Check for improvement."

"Sure. That'd be great." Beth knew the routine. Because it was a small elementary school, grade-level teachers worked together as a team sharing lesson-plan notes and progress reports. But Diane seemed more careful than usual with Corey. Was it because of Nick's position or Corey's transcripts?

Beth gestured toward the classroom. "He's working with Grace Cavanaugh right now. And Thomas Clark has taken Corey under his wing, too. They're all tablemates in the classroom."

"Good." Diane gave her a nod. "Good pairings there."

Beth wanted to roll her eyes. That was why she'd placed Corey at their table. "I thought so."

Diane nodded again. "Okay, then, I'm heading home. We'll meet soon."

"Sure thing." Beth slipped back into the art room.

"Miss Ryken, can you help us?" Gracie's hand was in the air with a tube of paint. "We can't get this open."

Beth popped the plastic top and handed it back. Both kids had donned aprons. Each one held a paintbrush.

Corey looked nervous as he stared at the blank white paper clipped to a tabletop easel.

Beth stood next to him and stared, too.

Corey looked at her, his eyes unsure.

"Let it fly, Corey."

"I don't know what to make."

Gracie was busy painting big red flowers.

Corey seemed too tentative. He did fine coloring preprinted pictures like the tall-ship work sheets in class, but the blank page intimidated him. Was that the result of his previous school making too much of the dark pictures the boy drew?

"Sometimes playing with the colors creates something special all by itself. Give it a try."

Corey thought about that a moment and then dipped his brush into Gracie's red paint. He slathered the paper and then rinsed the brush to try another color. Blue.

"There you go." Beth patted his shoulder. "Nice."

Corey looked at her again and smiled.

"You got it, Corey. Now have fun with it." Maybe he'd paint what was inside his heart.

Beth made her rounds, helping other kids and doling out encouragement. But she made her way back to Corey, curious.

"Wow!" She stared at his painting and smiled. "That's beautiful."

Corey had made a sloppy rainbow that ran off the page, but it arched over a corner painted black. None of the white paper showed. He'd filled it all with color. Did it mean something good? Beth couldn't help but think it did.

"You can have it."

Beth hesitated in accepting. Teacher mode, Diane had said. Her kids made pictures for her all the time. She had a slew of them in her desk. But this one was special. Like the boy in front of her. "What about your dad? He might like it, too."

Corey shrugged and looked away.

Beth regrouped. She didn't want to hurt the boy's feelings by refusing. Nick wouldn't mind, would he? "Thank you, Corey. I know right where it'll go."

His eyes brightened. "Really?"

"Really. Would you like to make another one?"

"Nope." Corey gathered up his brushes and headed for the sink. "I'm done."

Beth checked her watch. Still another forty-five minutes to go. "Corey, would you like to help me? Be my go-for?"

The boy looked thoughtful a moment. "What's a gopher?"

Beth smiled. "Go for things the other kids might need."

He nodded. "Okay."

"All right."

By the time Beth checked her watch again, it was time to pack up. Corey had been a good helper as they cleaned up spilled paint and passed out more paper.

Every errand she sent the boy on within the room had turned into a game of timing. Could he shave his last errand time down in seconds without running? Corey had laughed and fast-walked his way through tables and chairs. When stumped, he'd ask Gracie where to find something. The kid was sharp.

Parents filtered into the art room oohing and aahing over their kids' projects. Beth looked at Corey's. It wasn't quite dry but should be by the time they left. She'd have it framed.

Something told her this little step was huge. And her heart nearly burst with pride when she realized she'd been part of it.

Nick pulled into the Rykens' driveway. After a long workweek, he looked forward to his upcoming days off. He'd settle into the house he'd bought, mow the lawn and maybe shop for homeowner gadgets to stock the garage. Plus, he'd have time to get reacquainted with his son.

He rubbed his chin as the familiar feeling of panic shot through him quicker than a bullet. What kind of father was he to be afraid of his own son?

He slipped out of his patrol car and shrugged off his stupid fears. He was a grown man and a cop used to facing some pretty mean customers; he could do this. He'd been reading with Corey every night without making a dent of improvement that he could see. His boy couldn't read and Nick didn't know how to teach him. He sure hoped Beth had solutions stuffed up her pretty sleeves.

Charging the steps, Nick halted from stepping close enough to knock on the door. The windows were open to let in the unusually warm April evening breeze. He could hear Beth talking to Corey.

He could see them at the dining room table. The soft glow of the overhead light made Beth's blond hair shine. It looked silky and real. But then, it might come from a bottle for all he knew. His wife had colored her hair, but something about Beth made him think she didn't. He watched as she raised a good-sized card. Corey made the sound of the vowel combination and Beth smiled and then moved on to the next card.

That sunny smile of hers did things to him. He'd made the mistake of letting Susan get to him too fast, before he'd even had a chance to think. He'd never make that mistake again.

He stepped closer and knocked.

"Come in." Beth's voice.

Nick stepped inside, nodded and looked at his son. "Hey, bud."

Corey looked up. "Hey."

"Well, that's it for tonight. Good job, Corey."

"I'll get my stuff." Corey glanced at him as if trying to gauge how fast he should move.

"We've got time." Nick watched his boy relax and head for the kitchen. Nick slipped into a chair facing Beth. "So? What's the verdict?"

Beth pulled out a thin three-ring binder and slid it across the table toward him. "Here's your lesson plan."

He flipped open the cover. "My what?"

"Reading exercises to do with Corey. Have him

tell you a short story, you write it down and then have him read it back. As he improves, lengthen the story. Stuff like that in addition to regular reading. I've got a checklist for you so that you can keep track of what you've done. Nursery rhymes are a great tool, and remember, repetition is a good thing."

Nick ran a hand through his hair. She'd put a lot of work into this, but then, she was used to this stuff. He wasn't. "Thanks, I think."

She smiled and his stomach flipped. "You'll be okay."

Corey returned with his backpack, and Mary followed with two foil-covered plates.

"Wow, dinner again?" Nick accepted the gifts with gratitude.

"Yes, and some cookies." Mary gave Corey's shoulder a squeeze. "Did you show your dad the gift you made?"

Corey's eyes widened. "No."

Nick tipped his head. "What gift and for who?"

"Miss Ryken." Corey stared at his feet.

Nick glanced at Beth.

She set a big piece of thick paper on the dining room table. "Corey painted this at class tonight."

Nick took in the colors. It looked like every other kid's painting he'd seen hanging in a classroom. So? "That's great, bud."

Beth glared at him.

What?

Beth knelt so she was eye level with Corey. "I'll get this framed and then when you come back we'll pick out a place to hang it. Sound good?"

His boy nodded.

Nick felt as if he'd missed something here. It was just a painting. All kids painted, right? He tried to remember pictures from Corey hanging on their apartment walls and couldn't.

Susan hadn't framed any of Corey's colorings. Neither had he. They might have stuck a couple on the fridge of their old apartment, but other than that, not a big deal was made. Another should-have-but-didn't.

Mary patted Corey's arm. "Have a good time with your dad. We'll see you in a few days."

"Okay." Corey looked wary.

Nick rubbed his jaw. He had the next three days off.

Tomorrow was Friday and then the weekend spanned before him with no real plans made. He'd have to come up with something they could do together. His fingers gripped the binder Beth had made. He'd need more than this to keep them busy. "Thanks, Mary, and thank you, Miss Ryken."

"Why don't you call her Beth, like Mary does?" Corey looked up at him.

"Because she hasn't asked me to. And you'll call her Miss Ryken, too—is that understood? She's your teacher."

"Yeah, but—"

"And Mary should be Mrs. Ryken."

Beth came away from the dining room table. She wore faded jeans and a baggy T-shirt that hid her curves. "My mom told him it was okay to call her Mary."

"I'd prefer he didn't."

"Really, Nick, it's too confusing if he calls us both by our last names. Mary is fine for me," Beth's mother piped up.

Nick nodded. Mary's argument made sense. But he didn't want his son getting too comfortable on a first-name basis with his teacher and tutor. What if he made the mistake of calling her that in school? Could lead to trouble. Corey didn't need any more trouble.

The same went with him, too.

Beth's face softened as she studied him. The hum of attraction between them wasn't a good thing, either.

Without looking away from him, she said, "Corey, you better do as your dad says."

Corey looked from Beth to him and then back at Beth.

Nick felt like a heel for insisting. "For now, it's Miss Ryken."

"Yes. For now," Beth repeated.

Nick had a plate in one hand and the binder in

the other, so he nodded. "Good night and thanks. Let's go, bud."

"Good night."

Once in the patrol car with their goods in the backseat, Nick finally asked, "So how'd it go?"

Corey shrugged.

"We've got to work on this reading thing now, son. We can't let it go."

"Why?"

Nick didn't answer right away. He didn't want to threaten the boy with being held back. It was up to him as the parent to agree. Nick wouldn't, but what if Beth was right about it helping Corey instead of hindering him? Nick had already made so many mistakes.

"Dad?"

"Let's just work on it, okay?"

"Okay." Corey slumped lower.

Nick drove the rest of the way in silence. Yeah, sure, they were going to do real well the next few days.

Once they were inside their two-bedroom home, Corey went straight to his room. Nick went to his and changed out of his uniform. Nick met Corey in the kitchen. They both wore pajama bottoms and T-shirts.

"What do you say we watch a little sports and then read a book before bed." Nick nuked the plate Mary had given him. "Are you hungry?"

Corey nodded.

"Want more dinner?"

Corey shrugged and went to the cupboard. "I want cereal."

Nick watched his son grab a bowl and milk from the fridge all while he waited for the beep from the microwave. Silently they brought their dishes to the table. Nick peppered his food while Corey poured milk on his breakfast of champions.

"How was school today?" Nick couldn't stand the silence.

"Okay." Corey crunched on a mouthful of cereal.

"Do you like it here?"

Corey's eyes widened. "Yeah."

"Do you miss Grandma and Grandpa?"

Another crunch, but much slower this time. Corey looked as if he was searching for the right way to answer that question.

"It's okay if you do." Nick wouldn't blame the kid if he wanted to go back. He wasn't exactly a barrel of laughs and highly doubted he'd be up for any Father of the Year medals.

"I like it here," Corey said.

Nick nodded, satisfied with the boy's conviction. "Yeah, me, too."

The next day, Beth agreed to keep Corey in the classroom after school, where Nick would pick him up. She wondered what had happened to the boy.

He tried so hard to get the vowel sounds right and to read, she thought his head might explode. Like right now. Corey stared at the page with bulging eyes.

"I'm never going to get this." The seven-year-old pushed away his practice work sheets with frustration, knocking a book to the floor with a clap.

"Sure, you will. You're doing great."

Corey shook his head and tears threatened.

Beth tipped her head. She had an itchy feeling this wasn't about reading. "What's wrong, Corey?"

The boy wiped his nose with his sleeve. "I don't want to live with Grandma and Grandpa."

Beth's stomach tightened. Surely Nick wasn't considering that. "Has your dad said that you have to?"

More sniffling. "If I don't learn to read, he's going to send me back."

That couldn't be true. Still, Beth let the breath she'd been holding out slowly. "What makes you think so?"

Corey shrugged. "I just know."

Beth didn't know Nick well enough to assure the boy that wasn't going to happen. Was Nick pushing his boy too hard? Was she? Maybe that binder she'd made had scared both of them.

Beth studied the seven-year-old. "What do you and your dad like to do together?"

Corey shrugged.

"Come on, there must be something."

"We watch baseball on TV sometimes."

Beth smiled. LeNaro High School happened to have a very good baseball team. Their opening home game was tomorrow afternoon, too. "Anything else?"

"Dad likes to mow the lawn."

Beth chuckled. "Yeah?"

"I went with him to buy a new mower. He said when I was older, he'd show me how to mow."

That didn't sound like a man ready to pack his son off to the grandparents', but then, she wasn't sure.

"Okay, back to work. Your dad's going to be here soon." Beth scooted to get comfortable on the small seat and stretched her legs out under the table. She grabbed a book of silly poems with corresponding pictures that were equally ridiculous. "I think you might like these."

She read a couple short ones, glad to hear Corey laugh as he listened and followed the pictures. Poetry was a good place for phonics, too. Hearing the beats and rhythm of the words made them less intimidating. At least she hoped so, for Corey's sake.

After only a few minutes, a soft knock at her open classroom door jerked Beth's attention away from Corey. Nick stood tall in the doorway wearing jeans and a charcoal-colored long-sleeved shirt. He looked great. Major-league great.

Couldn't she look at the guy without her pulse reacting?

The corners of his lips curved into a semblance of a smile. "Hey."

"You should do that more often," Beth said before thinking.

"What's that?"

Might as well complete the blunder she'd started. "Smile."

He tipped his head and then looked at his son. "Hey, bud, how'd you do?"

Beth glanced at Corey.

"Okay." The boy had a thoughtful expression on his face.

She should tell Nick what Corey had told her and find out if it was true, find out how hard Nick was pushing, but she couldn't do that in front of the boy. Still, it sounded as if they needed something fun to do together. Something where they could connect. "I understand you both like baseball."

Both males looked at her as if she'd stated the obvious.

Beth swallowed a laugh. "Well, I don't know what you two have planned for the weekend, but the LeNaro High School baseball team is playing at home tomorrow afternoon. Should be a good game, too, as they're playing against an equally tough team. If you're interested in going, I'll print off a schedule."

Nick smiled again and looked at Corey. "Sounds like fun. Would you like to go, bud?"

Corey shrugged. "Okay."

Beth got up and went to her desk to print off a schedule as promised.

"Miss Ryken, will you go, too?" Corey asked.

"Uhhh—" Beth stuttered, knowing she should refuse, but the words stuck in her throat.

"Corey, I'm sure Miss Ryken has other plans." But Nick Grey had a hopeful look on his face, too. Hoping she'd refuse or agree, Beth wasn't sure.

"Please?" Corey begged.

How could she refuse those eyes?

"If you're not busy, it'd be great if you'd come with us." Nick looked sincere but guarded.

She bit her bottom lip. She needed to talk to him about his son anyway, his previous school's reports, his worries. Surely there'd be a moment to do that without making a big deal of it. And not in front of Corey.

Who was she trying to kid? Beth wanted to go, and she wanted Nick to want her to go, too. "Okay, yeah, sure."

Relief shone from Nick's eyes. "Great, do you want us to pick you up?"

Beth backpedaled a little as she handed Nick the

sports schedule. "I'll meet you there. It's an easy walk from the house."

"Okay, we'll see you tomorrow, then. Corey, do you have your stuff?"

The boy shouldered his backpack. "Yup."

"See you tomorrow." Beth breathed easier.

This was a harmless afternoon baseball game. Sure, she could wait until teacher-parent conference night, but Nick needed to know what worried his son now. A child under stress couldn't focus and learn. And they desperately wanted Corey to learn.

It wasn't as if it was a date or anything. She'd stick to teacher mode and they'd meet at a school function. Beth didn't date men in law enforcement. Tomorrow she'd make that clear to Nick. He deserved to know where she stood, and Beth didn't believe in playing games.

Straightening her classroom before calling it a day, Beth reassured herself that it'd be okay. Tomorrow would turn out fine. But she looked forward to the baseball game a little too much to really believe it.

Chapter Five

Nick made his way to the bleacher stands near the high school baseball field with Corey in tow. Players warmed up, and a few family members were already bundled on the bench seats in anticipation of the game. The day was sunny but cool. He'd be surprised if the temperatures climbed out of the fifties.

No sign of Beth yet, so Nick looked around.

The nearby concession stand opened its rolltop door with a rattle and snap, letting out the smell of freshly brewed coffee. This was small-town living at its best. The high school wasn't big by any means, but obviously the community rallied around it. An open concession stand manned by volunteers proved that.

He stared at the rolling hills dotted with orchards that lay beyond the sports fields. He thought of a show he used to watch on TV as a kid. Even then they were reruns, but Nick loved Sheriff Andy Taylor, who always had the right answer and time for his son. That was what Nick wanted.

He wanted Corey to grow up in a place where he could get involved in sports and the community. A place where they'd know people on a first-name basis. A place where they'd both belong, like Mayberry. Did he ask too much?

"There's Miss Ryken." Corey pulled on his sleeve.

Nick gave Beth a wave.

She waved back.

Beth had dressed for a chilly day in jeans and a jacket and a LeNaro Loons baseball cap. Her long hair had been pulled back into a ponytail, making her look young. He was pushing thirty-three, and if he hadn't known she taught second grade, he'd think she was college aged at best.

The closer she got, the better he could see that she didn't wear a trace of makeup. Young and unspoiled came to mind. Gawking at her, he felt stale and jaded. As if he'd been thrown in the dryer too long without a softener sheet.

Beth was fresh air and sunshine.

Did she have any idea how beautiful she was? Maybe she did and didn't care. She seemed comfortable in her skin. Being out and about without makeup was something his late wife would never have done. She had to look perfect even if they were only headed to the grocery store.

Beth smiled. "Have you been waiting long?"

Nick couldn't take his eyes off her. "We just got here."

Beth raised a woolen blanket draped over her arm. "I brought reinforcements. It can get pretty cold sitting on those metal bleachers."

He pushed aside sudden thoughts of snuggling close. "Would you like some coffee? Smells like it was just brewed."

"Sure." Beth gave him that sunny smile that hit him like a Mack truck.

Nick looked down at his son. "Corey, what about you? Do you want some hot chocolate?"

Corey wasn't listening. He waved to another little kid.

"Want to play catch?" the little boy hollered.

"Can I, Dad?"

Nick glanced at Beth. "Do you know that kid?"

Beth nodded. "That's Thomas Clark, Corey's tablemate at school. He's a good boy."

Nick nodded. "Stay where I can see you, okay, bud?"

Corey took off without another word, leaving him very aware of and alone with Miss Ryken. He gestured for Beth to take the lead to the concession stand.

The short woman behind the counter scanned him with interest before focusing on Beth. "So what brings you out to Jared's game before the finals?"

"Julie, this is Nick Grey. You remember, his son, Corey, is a new student in my class."

Julie reached out to shake his hand. "Nice to meet you, Nick. And your boy's a sweetie. Perchance do you like to sail?"

"Hmm, never done it." Nick wasn't sure what that had to do with anything.

Beth gave the woman a pointed look before turning to him. "Julie is the other second-grade teacher and Jared is her stepson. He plays third base."

"My husband and I sail. Beth goes with us at the end of the school year. It's sort of a tradition."

Nick nodded, still not sure what that had to do with him. "Great."

"We'll take two large coffees," Beth said.

"Sure thing." Julie gave him another once-over and then winked at Beth. "Inviting a guest is also somewhat of a tradition. So give it some thought."

"Ah, yeah sure." Nick paid for the coffee while Beth doctored hers with creamer and sugar.

Her cheeks were rosy pink. She was fresh faced, all right. But did her skin feel as soft as it looked?

Once seated on the folded blanket with steaming cups of coffee, Beth turned toward him. "Sorry about that."

He played dumb, which wasn't hard. "About what?"

"Julie and the sailing…" Beth waved it away.

"Was that an invitation, then?"

She looked flustered. "Yeah, but that's a long way away. Actually, I was hoping to talk to you about Corey."

Nick's stomach tightened as he took a sip of black coffee. "Everything okay?"

"I'm not sure. Corey's afraid you'll send him back to his grandparents if he doesn't read well."

Nick choked on the hot coffee. The woman didn't beat around the bush. "Where would he get that idea?"

Beth shrugged. "Corey told me in confidence, so please keep it under your hat. But I thought you should know because he's stressing about it. He's pushing himself pretty hard."

Nick nodded, but his gut felt as though it'd been shredded. He'd left Corey behind before, so it only stood to reason that his son didn't trust him not to do it again. He'd been pushing the reading exercises hard at home, too.

"You okay?" Beth's voice was soft, her cornflower-blue eyes even softer.

"I didn't tell him about being held back, so he must have concluded…" Nick ran a hand through his hair.

He spotted Corey playing catch. Someone had given him a small glove to use. His little guy had so much riding on those seven-year-old shoulders.

He shifted toward Beth. "I think Corey wanted you to come today because he's not easy around me anymore. He walks on eggshells, and maybe that's why. He thinks I'll leave him. I don't know what to do about it. He talks to you. Got any suggestions?"

Beth stirred her coffee with the little wooden stick. "Maybe what you need is something fun to do together. Find some interests in common."

Right now that interest was Beth Ryken. Corey liked her, and so did Nick. Maybe too much.

He raised his cup of coffee to her. "Like today— thanks. Maybe we can do this again."

Her eyes widened with alarm.

He'd just asked her out.

Time to be blunt, too. Before she got the idea he was trying to hit on her. "Look, Miss Ryken. I'd be a liar if I said I didn't find you attractive, but I'm in no place to get involved right now. I didn't mean for that to sound like a date."

She smiled at him without looking the least bit offended. Amazing woman. "That's good, because I don't date cops."

"Because of your father?"

Her eyes narrowed. "I saw what it did to my mom. And me when he didn't come home."

Nick nodded. Being the wife of a man in law enforcement wasn't easy. He'd seen the toll it had taken on his own mom. His parents had probably split because of it.

And then there was Susan's reaction to his job.

Beth seemed made of stronger stuff. Maybe she was and that was why she wanted no part of a cop's life. Beth knew her limitations.

Susan hadn't.

At first his wife had been enamored with the idea of him being an undercover cop. But they'd eloped only weeks after meeting, and then the reality of his late-night shifts sank in and she complained. A lot. He wasn't home enough. She got pregnant right away with Corey and everything took a dive from there.

Still, the Ryken women had made it through okay. They seemed well-adjusted, except for maybe Beth's refusal to give a cop a chance. But then, maybe that was wiser still and completely understandable.

"So how'd you and your mom get through it?"

Beth shrugged. "Church and friends, mostly."

"Were you and your mom always churchgoers?"

Beth nodded. "For as long as I can remember."

"That's good. I want that for Corey. He needs to grow up in a good church and know how to live a Christian life. I've been a poor example for a man of faith. I put God on the back burner for a while."

Beth's eyes widened. "And now?"

"Now I want Him front and center."

"Easier said than done, huh?"

Nick nodded.

"Don't worry, you're a better example than you realize."

Her words soothed, and he clung to them. "I hope you're right."

"Your son's a good boy, Mr. Grey. A little withdrawn maybe, but there's a gentle politeness there, too. He tests the waters with kids in his class before putting himself out there all the way. I'd guess he gets that from you."

"Yeah, maybe." Perceptive woman. He'd learned the hard way that what glittered wasn't always gold. Especially with Susan. She'd seemed so perfect in the beginning, but then they hadn't really known each other. Once married, that became all too clear.

The ball game started, so Corey made his way back into the bleachers and sat next to Beth as if he belonged there. As if he belonged to her. But the boy smiled at him. "Thanks, Dad."

Nick leaned forward. "For what?"

Corey shrugged. "Coming here."

"You're welcome." He glanced at Beth.

She gave him a soft smile that made him rethink his comment about not getting involved. What Beth had said was dead-on. He needed to find ways to share fun experiences with his boy if he hoped to knit their torn relationship back together. Maybe even make it stronger.

Still, there was no doubt Beth's presence had helped. Corey relaxed around her, and Nick wished some of that ease would rub off toward him. Maybe it would, in time.

For now, Beth made a good buffer between them. They needed her. In fact, they both might need Beth Ryken for a whole lot more than simply a reading tutor.

As the game wore on, Corey went back to playing catch with Thomas. Beth watched the clouds roll in and smother the sun.

She shivered. "This is why I don't come to many early-season games. I end up freezing."

"Here, use the blanket." Nick scooted off their woolen cushion and helped her pull it up around her shoulders.

"Thanks. You want half?" she asked before she'd considered sitting that close to him.

He cocked one eyebrow at her as if she'd lost her mind. "No. I'm fine."

Maybe she had, considering her speech about not getting involved. She wrapped the blanket tighter, and yet part of her was disappointed that he hadn't taken her up on her offer. He'd be warm to lean against.

And Nick was a man of faith, he'd said. Maybe that was why she'd connected with him on a level other than simple attraction. They had God in common.

She'd meant what she'd said about not dating

cops. Not that many had asked. A state trooper she'd met at a friend's wedding had once asked her out, but she'd declined his offer. She'd made a personal vow never to marry a police officer. But in the case of the state trooper, there'd been no spark.

She glanced at Nick. A shiver of excitement shot up her spine that had nothing to do with the cold. Sparks didn't begin to cover their mutual attraction.

Nick had admitted to finding her attractive. Sedate-sounding words, but she'd seen the fire in his eyes when he'd said it. As a woman, she found that look super gratifying. As a woman with a brain, she knew that look was as good as a red-flag warning.

Beth had few regrets in her life and she planned to keep it that way. Losing her father early in her teens made her realize how short life could be, so she played it safe. She thought long and hard before jumping in and weighed the consequences of each decision.

Her dad would never walk her down the aisle or hold her first child. Wonderful moments she'd miss all because what should have been a routine traffic stop ended with her father dead.

She glanced at Nick again. Falling for a guy like him could be the biggest regret of her life. *If* she let it happen. She wouldn't deny the desire to help him with his son. If she could legitimately get Corey ready enough for a fighting chance in third grade, then she could step away.

"Hi, Beth." Thomas's mom climbed the bleachers to sit in front of them.

"Sandy." She forced a smile that usually came with ease.

"And this must be Corey's dad. Hi, I'm Sandy Clark." She extended her hand along with a good dose of interest. "My boy's been talking nonstop about his new friend, Corey."

"Nick Grey." He accepted her handshake.

"Welcome to the area. We're going out for pizza after the game and would love it if you joined us. Thomas would be thrilled."

Surprise registered on Nick's face before he nodded agreement. "Thanks. Corey would like that."

"Great. We'll see you at Jemola's Pizza and Wings. Beth knows where it's at." Sandy gave them both a big smile and left.

Nick turned toward her. "Please say there's a Mr. Clark."

Beth laughed at the panicked look in his eyes. "Yes. Well, no, not anymore. They split up last year and share custody of Thomas."

"You've got to go with us," Nick pleaded.

Beth tipped her head and teased, "Don't tell me a tough guy like you is afraid?"

He nodded fast. "Did you see the glint in that woman's eyes?"

Beth laughed again.

Oh, she'd seen it, all right, and her hackles had risen because of it. They shouldn't have, though. Sandy Clark was a nice woman and solid mom. "You could do worse."

Nick gave her a long look. "I could do better."

Her heart pounded harder. She opened her mouth to remind Nick about how wrong for each other they were, but nothing came out. Diane's advice to stay in teacher mode rang through Beth's brain. Why had she said that, anyway?

He gave her a boyishly crooked grin that made her stomach flip. "Hey, all I'm looking for is friendship. No worries, okay? Come with us."

"Okay." Beth wanted to believe she'd agreed to go because of her weakness for pizza, but she knew better. Her weakness was all about Nick.

Once seated inside the pizza shop around a red-and-white-checkered table, Beth perused the menu.

"Pizza or wings?" Nick peered over her shoulder. "Which do you prefer?"

She fought the urge to lean back and into him. "Both."

"Then we'll get both." Nick's voice was low and soft.

Beth was an idiot to confuse an order of pizza

and wings with an endearment, but somehow Nick had made it sound that way. She quickly focused on Corey. "What do you like on your pizza?"

Corey looked thoughtful and then confused. "Huh?"

Beth smiled. "What kind of pizza do you like?"

The boy shrugged. "Pepperoni, right, Dad?"

"That's right." Nick looked pleased with his son's cheerfulness. "Good call coming here."

Thanks to Sandy. Beth bit back jealousy. "Yeah, it was."

"Hey, Beth, Mr. Grey." Her school's counselor stopped by their table.

"Hi, Diane."

"Try their specialty pizza today. It's barbecue chicken and awesome."

"Thanks." Why did Beth feel as if she'd been caught doing something wrong?

"I like pepperoni," Corey said.

"You do? Well, that's good, too." Diane smiled and then turned her attention toward Nick. "Looks like you guys are settling in."

"We are."

Corey's attention was caught by the arrival of Thomas and his mom.

"Thanks for getting a table. This place fills up pretty fast after games." Sandy slipped into a seat right next to Nick. "Hi, Diane, do you want to join us?"

Diane tapped on the tabletop. "Oh, no, my husband's waiting for me in the car. Thank you. Nice to see you."

"See you Monday." Beth was glad Sandy had shown up. She didn't need Diane thinking she and Nick were an item. Not so soon after being advised to stay in teacher mode.

Corey stared at Thomas's mom but didn't say a word.

Beth glanced at Nick to see if he'd introduce his son. When he didn't say anything, she stepped up. "Corey, this is Mrs. Clark."

Sandy smiled. "Hello."

"Hi." Corey's voice was barely audible.

"Mom, can we have some quarters for games?" Thomas held out his hand.

Sandy dug in her purse.

Nick stood and placed his hand on Corey's shoulder. "Come on, bud, let's check out those games."

The boys followed Nick to the corner by the door where an ancient pinball machine stood proud with lights flashing. There was also one of those claw machines packed with stuffed animals that begged to be played with and lost.

Beth watched Nick instruct the boys.

He might not realize it, but Nick was pretty good with kids. He didn't try too hard to sound interested, nor did he talk down to them. Kids saw right through a patronizing tone.

"So, Beth, are you and Nick Grey seeing each

other?" Sandy asked after they'd given the waitress their order while the boys continued to play.

"No." Beth shifted. Seeing the gleam in Sandy's eyes made her want to stretch the truth.

Sandy's eyes narrowed. "Oh?"

Beth came clean, partially. "My mother watches Corey after school."

"Ahh. Nick seems like a nice guy."

"He is." Beth's impression of Nick had been way different than *nice* that day he'd showed up in her classroom. He had an edge to him. A good attribute for a cop.

Beth sipped her pop.

Sandy glanced toward the pinball machine. "So what's his story? Divorced?"

"Widowed." Beth figured that was common enough knowledge to repeat. Still, she didn't like giving Sandy any pointers. Or encouragement.

"Awww, that's too bad." Sandy's eyes had softened but they didn't look a bit sorry. More like relieved that there wasn't a Mrs. Grey lurking in the background.

"Yeah." What else could she possibly say?

"Hey, Beth!"

Beth looked up to see her friend hurrying toward her. "Eva!"

They quickly embraced, and then Eva looked around the crowded restaurant. "Wow. Not many tables open."

"Join us," Beth said, and then glanced at Sandy to see if she'd mind.

"Adam is with me, along with Ryan and Kellie. You sure there's room?"

"We'll make room." Sandy smiled and pulled a small table for two that was empty toward their larger one. She welcomed the additional people and yet Beth didn't think it was about "the more, the merrier."

Easier to corner Nick in a group. Really! What was wrong with her? If she didn't want him, she shouldn't care if someone else might.

Tamping down her venomous thoughts, Beth made the introductions as they all pitched in to help Sandy gather chairs.

"Hello." Nick had returned with the two boys. He took the increased size of their party in stride, save for the raised eyebrow he gave her.

Beth did the honors. "This is Nick Grey and his son, Corey. They recently moved to LeNaro and Corey's in my class."

Eva reached out her hand. "And this is my fiancé, Adam, my brother Ryan and his fiancée, Kellie."

After a quick round of small talk, everyone sat down. Beth noticed that Sandy had managed to scoot next to Nick again. She shrugged it off and concentrated on Eva. "You're getting close."

Eva grinned. "Two weeks until the wedding. I can hardly wait."

"Me neither." Adam brought Eva's hand to his lips.

Eva brushed him aside. Her cheeks were pink but she beamed with joy.

"The cherry blossoms will be wide-open by then," Ryan added with a look of such sweetness toward Kellie that Beth's heart twisted.

She'd once had hopes of capturing Ryan's notice, but Kellie was perfect for him. And Beth was happy for them all. Really, she was, but when would true love happen for her?

As if her eyes had a will of their own, she glanced at Nick.

He gave her that crooked grin that wasn't much of a smile at all.

She smiled back. He looked bored out of his mind. From Sandy's chatter or the table talk about cherry farming, Beth wasn't sure. Still, meeting new people was good for him, considering his newness to town.

Eva's smile grew wider as she glanced at Nick and then back at her. "So, Beth, have you thought about who you're bringing to the wedding?"

As they left the pizza shop, rain poured from the sky with no sign of letting up. Under the red-and-white awning, Nick turned to Beth. "We'll give you a ride home."

She looked as if she might argue but nodded. Her house was only a few blocks away, but she'd be soaked through if she walked home.

He watched Beth wave goodbye to her friends as the two couples climbed into a huge blue pickup. They were nice people. Sandy and her son raced to their car, too. Beth was right about her; he could do a lot worse, but Sandy Clark held no interest for him.

Corey didn't seem impressed, either. He'd barely spoken to the woman.

"Ready to run?" He clicked the remote to unlock his small SUV. He'd traded in his car before the move, after hearing about the winters up north. He looked forward to putting the four-wheel drive to use. Maybe he and Corey could learn to ski.

"Ready." Beth reached for Corey's hand.

His son took it as naturally as if he'd been holding hands with Beth forever. But then, she was his teacher. Little kids must be used to that sort of thing.

They made a dash for the car.

Beth pulled open the back door for Corey and waited while he climbed into his booster seat.

She slipped into the passenger side with a squeal. "Rain just dribbled down my back."

They were soaked dashing for the car. And cold.

Beth shivered and then clenched her teeth to keep them from chattering.

"Corey, hand me that blanket," Nick said.

"I'm okay." Beth rubbed her arms.

"You'll be home before the heat kicks in." Nick wrapped the blanket around her shoulders. That small movement brought them into close proximity.

Close enough to kiss.

His gaze lingered on her full lips.

"Thanks." She sounded breathless.

He leaned back fast. "You're welcome."

The air inside his car hummed with more than the drone from the defroster on high. The scent of rain mixed with the softness of Beth's perfume had Nick's brain reeling.

Friendship. He'd said that was all he was looking for, but it sure wasn't all he wanted.

Nick glanced at Corey through the rearview mirror. The kid's eyes were wide but not wise. His boy couldn't possibly understand the currents of attraction swirling around them.

For Corey's sake, Nick wouldn't get involved with Beth. There was too much to lose if they suddenly broke up. Women could be vindictive when they wanted to be, and he wouldn't risk exposing Corey to any of that. Especially when he needed to concentrate on reading. The poor kid had had enough drama to last a lifetime.

Friendship. That was all he'd offer Beth until he knew his son had passed second grade. That was all he could handle until he knew for sure what kind of woman Beth proved to be.

Chapter Six

Sunday morning, Beth entered her small community church with her mom. Spotting Eva Marsh, Beth waved. And her friend made a beeline straight for her.

"Morning."

"So what's the deal with that redheaded guy who can't keep his eyes off you?" Eva kept her voice secret-sharing low.

Beth shook her head. "I thought you'd decided to attend your brother's church."

"We are, but we still like to visit. I grew up coming here."

Beth scanned the packed pews for her friend's outrageously handsome fiancé. He chatted comfortably with a crusty old farmer named Jim Sanborn. Although Adam was now a full-time cherry grower, he didn't fit that role today. Dressed in crisp gray slacks and a cotton sweater, Adam looked as urbane as when he'd first knocked on Eva's door over a year ago. Beth had been her roommate then, and she'd coaxed Eva to give Adam a chance. Now they ran Marsh Orchards together and would soon open a bed-and-breakfast to boot.

Eva poked her in the ribs with her elbow. "So? What gives with Nick Grey?"

"Nothing gives. His son is in my class and my mom watches Corey after school."

"And?"

"And that's it." That was all it should be.

"I don't believe you."

Beth never could pull one over on Eva. "He's a deputy sheriff."

"Oh." Eva wrinkled her nose.

She knew Beth's criteria. She also knew how much her father's death had affected her. Eva had been a strong friend through the tragedy. If not for Eva, Beth didn't know what she might have fallen into trying to cope with the loss.

"So…he's off-limits."

"Pretty much." Beth knew what it was like to wait at home and worry. She'd seen her mother do it most of her life. When Beth was old enough to understand the danger her father faced on the job, she had worried, too.

Working in a relatively safe place like Northern Michigan hadn't mattered in the end. They all had breathed easier after moving here, thinking the threat had been removed and her father was safe. But her dad hadn't been killed on the streets of suburban Detroit. He'd been shot on a lonely stretch of back road in Leelanau County and left for dead.

Eva squeezed her arm. "Well, your Mr. Grey just walked in the door and he's headed our way. Maybe he doesn't know he's on your do-not-touch list."

Nick's hair looked damp from a shower and he wore a long-sleeved navy shirt and jeans. Tall and lean, Nick wore jeans well. Even better than his sheriff's uniform.

"He knows." Beth took a deep breath.

Nick wanted to bring God onto the front burner of his life.

Even more reason to like the guy.

"Uh-huh." Eva gave her a doubtful look.

"Look, Nick doesn't want to get involved, either." With Corey's issues, moving to a new town with a new job, Nick had more things to concentrate on than her.

"And he told you that when? After you told him about your vow not to date policemen?"

Beth rubbed her forehead. Since when had Eva gotten so smart? "I don't know. Maybe."

And then Nick stood before them with Corey closing in right behind him. "Miss Ryken."

Beth smiled. "Mr. Grey." They still didn't call each other by first names. "Hi, Corey."

Eva's eyes held amusement before she extended her hand. "Nick, was it?"

He accepted it. "Yes. And you're Eva Marsh."

"Soon to be Eva Peecetorini. In fact, it…"

Beth gave her friend a pointed look. Would Eva get the hint not to invite Nick? They didn't need any matchmaking. If Beth wanted him to go, she'd ask him herself. She didn't need any help. Didn't want it, either.

"…is just a matter of waiting now." Eva smiled.

And Beth let out the breath she'd been holding.

"Congratulations." Nick nodded.

Eva barely contained the happiness that perked and gurgled within her, ready to bubble over on them. "Thanks. Nice to see you both again. Bye, Corey."

"Bye."

Beth watched Eva sidle up to her fiancé. The two were rarely far from each other for very long. The music started and folks scattered into their seats.

"After you." Nick gestured for her to lead the way.

They were going to sit together. And why shouldn't they? They were friends, right? Despite Eva's observation that Nick's gaze had lingered on her at the pizza shop, they were friends. They were adults, too. They could handle attraction for each other and not act on it.

Beth slipped into a pew next to her mom.

"Morning." Nick strategically placed Corey between them.

"Good morning, Nick. If you're not busy after church, why don't you and Corey come over for dinner?"

Beth felt the smile on her face freeze. Her mother hadn't said a thing about inviting the Greys for Sunday dinner. She'd been looking forward to an afternoon nap.

Nick glanced at her. "Thank you, but I don't think so...."

Corey turned toward his dad. "Can we, please?"

"I have more than enough, and homemade cookies are on tap for dessert. I made the dough this morning." Her mom knew how to twist the knife.

Nick hesitated.

Because of her. And that would never do, not when Corey wanted to come over. She faced Nick. "You can't turn down homemade cookies."

He gave her that crooked half smile. "What kind?"

"Peanut butter."

"My favorite."

Hers, too. Beth smiled.

He smiled back.

Were they kidding themselves to think they could maintain mere friendship? Nick needed to make summer arrangements for Corey soon. Then they'd hardly see each other. Save for maybe Sunday mornings.

Nick leaned forward. "I guess that settles it. We'll be there."

Beth ignored the flutter of excitement that zipped through her. This was going to be a long six weeks until summer break.

Throughout the worship service, Beth heard Nick's deep voice singing the songs as if he knew them. Proof that he'd been a churchgoer, as he'd said. Not that she had any reason to doubt him, but hearing him sing reassured her all the same.

When the kids were dismissed for children's church, Corey hesitated.

Beth leaned toward the boy. "You don't have to go, but you'll have more fun there than here. Do you want me to walk you down and then you can decide?"

The boy nodded and took her hand.

Beth glanced at Nick. "I'm going to go with him to check it out."

He gave his boy a reassuring nod. "It's okay, bud. See what you think." And then he looked at her and mouthed the words *thank you*.

Maybe she'd overstepped her place, but Beth got the feeling that Nick didn't expect Corey to go. And then Corey would miss out. She knew the children's program director and her aides. They'd take good care of the boy and maybe he'd make more friends.

As they descended the steps, Beth asked, "Did you go to church with your grandparents?"

"Sometimes."

"Did they have stuff for kids to do during service?"

Corey shook his head. This was clearly all new to him.

They entered the noisy lower level and Beth introduced Corey to the teenage co-teacher. "He's new to the area."

"Great." The girl gave Corey a wink. "We're going to have a snack first before we get started. Do you like animal cookies and juice?"

Corey nodded.

The girl offered her hand. "Follow me and I'll find a place for you."

Corey looked at Beth.

"I'll hang out for a little bit if you'd like to stay."

That satisfied. Corey went with the teenager and squished in between a couple other kids at the table.

After snack time and cleanup, it didn't take long for Corey to join in *their* form of singing. Beth watched for a few moments while the kids moved and wiggled to match the words of the song amid giggles and laughter.

Corey wiggled, too, and when he glanced her way, Beth gave him a wave and left for upstairs.

The minister was already into his message when she slipped in next to Nick.

He leaned close, sending a shiver through her. "He's okay?"

"Yeah, he's doing great."

Beth tried to focus on the sermon. Pretty hard to do with Nick next to her. Everything about him seemed magnified in the space of the pew. Her gaze strayed to his strong hands resting on long jean-clad thighs.

"God answers prayer," she heard the minister say. *"He doesn't always give us what we want, but He'll give us exactly what we need."*

Beth closed her eyes as those words hit her hard and took root. God knew what she wanted—a safe man to love and make a family with. But what if she needed something else?

"Try this one again." Nick had the sports page of the weekend paper open on the coffee table in the living room. He and Corey had been banished from helping in the kitchen.

Silence.

Nick glanced at Beth setting the table in the dining room. She wore a blue dress with white polka dots that skimmed the middle of her calves.

Tall and trim yet with full curves, Beth looked ultrafeminine and sort of old-fashioned, as if she'd stepped right out of the Dust Bowl era. She'd kicked off her sandals when they walked in the door and puttered around in her bare feet.

He liked watching her move.

His chest tightened as it hit him that this felt like home. Listening to Beth and her mom fixing a meal together lulled him into a relaxed, sleepy sort of place. Tempted to stretch out on the couch and close his eyes, he wondered how the Rykens would react if he did just that.

Only then he'd miss watching Beth.

He looked at his son. Corey's eyes were glued to the TV screen. There was work to be done, so he tapped the newspaper. "Come on, bud. It's about the Tigers, your favorite team."

Corey shrugged. "I don't want to read it."

Nick grabbed the remote and clicked off the television. This was their ritual. Nick brought out the books, and every night Corey said he didn't feel like reading. Nick insisted. Corey slumped and tried and stumbled and grew more discouraged until Nick couldn't stand it. So he'd take over and read the rest.

That probably wasn't what Beth had in mind when she'd given him books for his son to read. He thought about what Beth had told him yesterday. Corey was stressed. Somehow he had to put his boy's fears to rest without breaking Beth's confidence.

"Corey, look at me."

His son obeyed.

"We've got all summer to work on this, but the more progress we make now, the easier it will be. You want to be ready for third grade, right?"

Corey looked at him closely as if reading between lines, only he struggled there, too.

"Look, bud, would you rather repeat second grade?"

His son's eyes grew round with fear.

Nick hated scaring the boy but he needed to level with him.

"No...."

Nick nodded. "I don't want you to either, but we've got to work hard and show Miss Ryken you're ready to move on. Don't you think we should try?"

Corey nodded.

Nick had him. "I heard the third-grade teacher here is pretty tough."

"How do you know?" Corey responded with a look of pure skepticism.

Nick had lost him and thought quick. "Thomas's mom might have said something about it."

Corey narrowed his eyes even more and then glanced at Beth.

Nick closed the deal before his boy saw through the fib. "This is about getting you ready to learn big stuff next year. You're a smart kid and this is a hiccup we've got to cure."

"Okay." Corey sighed and pulled the paper close. "Will the Ti-eye…geerrrrs maaake the paaay-uh."

Nick cringed. "That's it. Take your time and sound it out. What do the Tigers do?"

"Play baseball. Play-offs?" Corey looked at him.

"Yeah. What do you think? Will they go this year?"

Corey grinned. "They better."

Nick ruffled his son's hair. "If they know what's good for them. Okay, let's get back to the article."

He spotted Beth standing in the dining room with a dish towel in her hands watching them. Their gazes locked and he saw the approval shining in her blue eyes. He got the feeling that he'd turned a corner with his son. Maybe with Beth, too.

"Dinner's ready," she said softly.

"Let's wash up, bud." Nick stood.

"Can we take the paper home with us?" Corey asked.

Nick could have given his son a bear hug but decided against it. Small steps required small reactions to keep them going. "Absolutely. After we make sure it's okay with Mrs. Ryken."

"We've read it. You can take the paper." Beth nodded. "Now hurry up. Mom and I are setting out the food."

Dinner smelled amazing and he wasted no time bustling Corey into the half bathroom to wash up.

Once they were seated around the table, Mary grabbed his hand. "Will you say the blessing?"

"Sure." Nick took Corey's hand and bowed his head. Beth sat across from him holding his son's other hand and her mom's. They made a tight circle around the table. "Thank You, Lord, for bringing us together. Please bless this food, and bless us as we place our trust in You. Amen."

Mary squeezed before letting go. "That was lovely."

Nick nodded. The words had sort of spilled out of him. He was grateful Beth was Corey's teacher and her mom lived right across the street from the school.

Even more grateful that they attended church and made good role models for his son. This move north was looking more and more like the right thing. And Corey might yet grow easier around him.

Nick didn't feel so lost. Not with the help he received from these two women. As he sat in the Ryken dining room spooning a healthy glop of mashed potatoes onto his plate, this felt like family. He glanced at Beth. She cut Corey's roast beef into smaller bites.

She'd make a great mom.

To Corey.

He banished the thought before it took root.

Nick needed a level of certainty in who Beth was before he could even think about pursuing her. This time, he'd know the woman inside and out before he'd allow one kiss between them. Then there was the mammoth obstacle of Beth's objection to his choice of career to consider. He couldn't promise her he'd always be safe. What had happened to Beth's father could happen to him.

But if God had truly brought them together as he'd prayed, then dating would fall into place at the right time. Or not at all.

Nick trusted his calling for law enforcement and he'd trust God to take care of preparing Beth's heart. If they were meant to be together, they would be.

Monday afternoon, Beth walked home from school with a new packet of reading material centered on sailing for Corey. The boy had worked well with Thomas on an essay assignment about tall ships. Corey had even completed a couple of answers.

The child had listened with rapt attention when Beth read a story about sailing ships and trade on

Lake Michigan during the eighteen hundreds. She wondered if Julie's invite to sail the Manitou Islands wasn't something that might work as further incentive for Corey. A reward to work toward that was tangible, instead of the fear of failing. She'd have to talk to Nick about it.

"I'm home." Beth kicked off her shoes, but silence greeted her.

"Mom? Corey?" She walked into the kitchen. The house was too quiet.

Then she peered out the windows into the backyard. Both her mom and Corey were on the grass playing with a small black-and-white terrier. A small dog with a very round belly.

Beth stepped outside onto the deck. "What's this?"

Her mom grinned. "Isn't she precious?"

Had her mom brought home a pregnant dog?

The little girl came right up to her, tail wagging. Beth crouched low and scratched behind the pooch's ears. "Where did she come from?"

"She followed me home from school," Corey said.

The dog responded to Corey's voice and went straight for him, climbing onto the boy's lap to lie down as if she'd finally found safe harbor. Just like the ships they'd read about today.

Beth couldn't believe the look of adoration that

little dog gave to Corey. She nuzzled under his hand, begging to be pet. "She's adorable."

And very, very pregnant. How many puppies did she carry and how much bigger could she possibly get before delivery? The dog wore no collar. Surely she belonged to someone. Or had someone dropped her off by the school because they didn't want to deal with puppies?

Beth clenched her teeth. How could anyone do something so horrible?

"She looks like a misshaped peanut," her mom said.

Beth laughed when the dog's ears perked up.

"Do you think Peanut is her name?" Corey said.

Again the dog looked up at Corey and then cuddled her head against him.

"It suits her, that's for sure." Beth had never seen a dog so enamored with a child before. As if Peanut had chosen Corey as her own and expected him to protect her. Provide for her.

What was Nick going to say?

"We gave her some milk-soaked bread that she lapped up pretty quick." Her mom brushed off her jeans and stood. "I think she might have been wandering awhile, but she's pretty clean. No fleas that I can see."

Maybe she'd been well cared for and gotten lost. Which meant her owners might be worried sick.

Beth took a deep breath. "Corey, we should find out if her owners are looking for her."

The boy's eyes clouded over. "How? Why would they lose her if they wanted to keep her?"

Good question. "I don't know, but anything can happen with a dog."

Corey cuddled her closer.

And Beth prayed there was no one looking for little Peanut.

By the time they heard Nick pull into the driveway, they'd eaten dinner and Beth had returned from a quick trip to the store for a bag of dry dog food. Tutoring Corey on his reading had gone out the proverbial window. They'd played and fawned over Peanut the entire evening. Beth would gather books about dogs—a new subject of interest for Corey.

After a quick knock on the door, Nick stuck in his head. "Hello?"

"Come in, Nick. We're in the living room," her mother called out.

Beth met Nick in the dining room. "We've got a surprise for you."

He cocked his eyebrow.

"Dad! Dad!" Corey had jumped to his feet. "This is Peanut. Can we keep her?"

Beth watched Nick's controlled expression. "She followed Corey home."

"Is that dog fat or is there something else going on?" Nick didn't look amused.

Corey grabbed his father's hand and pulled. "She's going to have puppies. Come here and feel. They're moving around inside."

Nick glanced at her with wide eyes while following his son into the living room. He sat on the couch where Peanut lay like a miniature beached whale.

Sure enough, something inside that rounded belly moved.

"See? Did you see that?" Corey jumped up and down.

"I saw it." Nick laid his hand on the dog's stomach and his expression grew more grim. He scratched under the dog's chin before standing back up.

The dog watched him.

"I don't know, Corey. She must have owners who are looking for her."

"But there's no collar." Corey's chin lifted defiantly.

And Beth intervened. "Nick, are you hungry?"

"There's a plate for you in the kitchen." Her mother started to get up from her chair.

Beth waved her to stay put. "I'll get it for him, Mom." She gave Nick a pointed look to follow her.

He glanced back at his son, who had sat down on the couch, and Peanut climbed into his lap.

"We can't keep that dog," he said.

Beth glared at him to keep quiet until they reached the kitchen. "Come on."

"Miss Ryken…"

She held up her hand to stop him. "Before you decide, that dog loves Corey. I've never seen anything like it."

"Maybe you and your mom can keep her here until I have a chance to find out if anyone's looking for her."

Beth nodded and popped the plate of leftovers into the microwave. "We can do that. Have fun getting her away from Corey, though."

Nick sat at the table and raked his hands through his short-cropped red hair. "What are we going to do with a dog?"

"With puppies." Beth grinned.

Hard-edged Nick was one big softy. He'd caved pretty quick. He gave her an exasperated look. "With puppies."

She set the warmed plate in front of him along with a tall glass of milk. "Maybe this little dog is Godsent."

"How do you figure that?"

She sat across from him and took a deep breath. "Well, I've been praying for you and Corey to find a common interest. Something other than reading that would bring you together daily. And look what showed up."

Nick looked surprised. "You prayed for me?"

"And Corey." Beth felt her face flush.

"That's good. Keep doing that." Nick briefly bowed his head before digging into his food.

Corey wandered into the kitchen with Peanut following him. "Can we keep her, Dad?"

Nick gave his son and the dog a long look. "First we have to see if anyone claims her. If not, then yes, bud. We'll keep her."

"Yippeeeee." Corey flew at his dad and hugged him.

Nick returned it with a fierceness that made Beth's eyes sting. She got the feeling Corey and his father hadn't embraced in a while.

Beth offered up a silent prayer of thanks.

Funny, but the message from the church service the day before came back with an interesting twist. *God answers prayer.* He might not give what's wanted but always delivers what's needed.

Nick and Corey needed this little dog.

Chapter Seven

Nick peeked in on Corey. His boy slept soundly with Peanut snuggled into his armpit. In that moment the dog opened her eyes and looked at Nick as if studying him. She had a pretty black face with a white streak down her nose and small swatches of tan on her cheeks. He might be crazy, but he got the distinct feeling the dog wanted to stay with them. Maybe it was the way the dog had latched on to Corey or the relaxed look on her face as if she'd finally made it home.

"I'll do my best to keep you, girl," Nick whispered.

That seemed to satisfy the dog. She shifted and snuggled her nose right back into the crook of Corey's arm.

He stepped back and closed his son's bedroom door partway. He couldn't leave that dog behind tonight at Beth's. Corey's eyes had welled with unshed tears and he just couldn't do it. So into the car Peanut had gone with tail wagging as she settled into his son's lap for the short ride home.

Mary had told him that when he dropped Corey off at school, he could also drop Peanut off at her house before Beth left. That way the dog would only be alone during the morning hours. She'd keep her until Nick picked up Corey, watching her in case of puppy delivery.

Nick's gut tightened. What did he know about dogs having puppies?

Absolutely nothing.

He scratched a quick note on his to-do list to call a veterinarian in the morning. There was a small vet office not far from their house. Maybe they'd know something about the little dog. If not, he'd run an ad in the paper to cover all bases.

He hoped nobody claimed the pooch. Corey was smitten and Nick hated the thought of having to pry Peanut from his son's arms. He prayed he wouldn't have to.

His phone rang and he picked up before the second ring. "Nick Grey here."

"Hi, it's Beth. Sorry to call so late—"

"Miss Ryken," Nick purred. "What's up?"

She laughed. "You can call me by my first name, you know."

"I know." He might need the distance, but he liked calling her by her teacher title.

"Well, then, *Mr. Grey,* you left your sheriff's hat here."

Nick glanced at the decorative hooks by the back door where he usually hung his hat. Empty. "Thanks for calling. I would have looked all over. I'm going to try to get Peanut to the vet's tomorrow and then I'll drop her by after your mom gets home."

"How'd she do?"

"She's snuggled up with Corey and they're sleeping."

"Good."

"Which reminds me." Nick ran his hand through his hair. "I've got to cover an overnight shift this Saturday night. The guy on duty's wife had a C-section this week. I hate to ask, but do you think your mom would watch Corey and Peanut at your place overnight?"

"Of course. It'd be fine. We'd love to have them both."

Nick breathed easy. He didn't doubt her. Beth's quick answer and upbeat tone spoke volumes. She cared for his son. A lot. "We didn't get much reading done tonight."

"We didn't either with the excitement over Peanut."

"Yeah, Peanut." Nick hoped they could keep her. "I'll try to get Corey back on track tomorrow night."

"You will."

Nick liked the confidence she had in him.

"In fact..." Beth stalled.

"What?"

"Corey has shown a marked interest in boats, and I go sailing at the end of the school year with the other second-grade teacher and her husband. Do you remember meeting Julie at the baseball game?"

He remembered. The woman had hinted at him going, too. Maybe Beth didn't want that. "You want to take Corey?"

"I thought it might be a good incentive to keep him focused on reading. Use the sailing trip as a reward for making progress. A reason not to quit trying."

"How big is this boat?"

"It's big enough for half a dozen adults and a couple kids for sure. Of course, I'd like you to come, too. So you'll feel comfortable with Corey's safety."

"Of course." Nick smiled.

She was so careful. Careful to reinforce that his invite was all about Corey. But he wondered...

"Is that a yes, then?"

He shifted his phone. "I'd say it is."

"Good. Well, I better let you go. We can talk more about the details another time."

"Yeah, sure." Nick wouldn't mind chatting a bit longer. "See you tomorrow."

"Good night, Nick." Beth's voice sounded soft, even hesitant as she called him by his first name for the first time.

He had to admit that he liked the sound of it coming from her. Even over the phone, the connection between them hummed to life. He scanned his empty kitchen and envisioned Beth setting the table for Sunday dinner here.

It was too soon, much too soon to go there.

"Good night, Beth."

By the end of the week, Beth had gone through several children's books about dogs having puppies with Corey. His reading had slowly improved after he'd finally nailed down some phonic rules. The boy's interest in the subject matter helped as well, but Beth knew they'd lose ground in keeping Corey focused when those pups were born.

Nick had reported that according to the vet, Peanut was in good health. A tangle of puppy heartbeats had showed up on the ultrasound. The vet believed she'd deliver sometime within the next two weeks. They were all on puppy watch.

A knock at the door brought Beth's nose out of the book she'd been trying to read. Peering through the window, she spotted Nick and Corey on the front porch with an overnight bag.

Tonight Nick was on patrol.

Beth hurried toward the door and opened it wide, stepping back. "Hey."

Nick carried in a duffel bag. Corey carried a bag of dog food. And Peanut trotted in behind them as if she owned the place.

Beth bent down and scratched the dog's ears. Then she glanced at the clock. It was six in the evening. Nick's shift started at seven and ended at seven in the morning. "Did you guys have dinner?"

"We ate before we came." Nick set the duffel on the couch. "Corey's clothes and pj's."

Beth nodded.

"Dad made spaghetti." Corey sat down on the floor next to Peanut. The dog had climbed into the middle of a pink-cushioned dog bed, compliments of her mother.

Beth glanced at Nick. "Wow. I'm impressed."

"Don't be. It's not hard to open a jar and boil water." He looked around. "Where's your mom?"

"She went to the store to buy stuff for breakfast. Mom wants it ready when you come to pick Corey up."

Nick shook his head. "She doesn't have to do that."

"I know, but try to tell her that."

"I have and it doesn't work." Nick referred to all the meals she'd sent home with him.

"Now you know what I live with." Beth tried to

get her mother to follow a sound budget that included a savings plan. She fought a losing battle.

"Walk me to the door?"

Beth glanced at Corey. "The Tigers are playing in Atlanta, if you want to turn on the TV. Mom had the game on before she left."

The boy nodded and grabbed the clicker. "Thanks, Miss Ryken."

"You're welcome."

Nick's gaze bore into hers. "Thank you for keeping him overnight. You've got the numbers?"

"Yes." Beth swallowed hard. Nick meant the phone numbers for Corey's grandparents. Just in case he didn't come home.

He looked so tall and foreboding in his sheriff's uniform, but Nick was lean enough to encourage someone to take a crack at him. Beth didn't like that. She didn't like the thought of him patrolling alone all night, either.

"I owe you, big-time," he whispered.

He'd paid her mom generously for her time tonight. Too much, Beth thought. She gave him a cheeky grin she didn't feel inside. "Yeah, you do."

He returned her quip with a lopsided grin. "Exact your payment, then."

Beth's stomach swirled and danced. Nick Grey could flirt when he wanted to. "Be careful tonight."

His eyes grew sober in an instant. "I'm always

careful. It's my job to be ready for anything and anticipate the worst."

Beth resisted the urge to touch him. She wanted to feel the iron strength of Nick's arms wrapped around her. Maybe smooth back that red hair of his.

She wrung her hands instead. "It's the *worst* that bothers me."

Nick stepped closer and grasped her hands, stilling them. For a minute, Beth thought she might get her wish, but instead of pulling her closer, Nick nodded. "I'll see you in the morning, Beth."

"Okay." He hadn't promised, but the confidence in his voice helped. A little.

This was the reason she didn't want to fall for Nick. She hated the gnawing fear in the pit of her stomach at the thought of him roaming dark back roads in the wee hours with backup miles away.

He let go of her hands. "Good night, Corey. Listen to Mary and Miss Ryken."

"Sure." Corey nodded, but his gaze was fixed on the game.

Nick gave her a wink and then left.

Beth closed the door behind him and then leaned against it. Had her dad relaxed too much up here? Was that what had gotten him killed? Maybe he hadn't expected the worst when he approached the car he'd pulled over for speeding. Maybe her dad had been tired that night.

"Corey?" Beth's stomach turned over.

"Yeah?"

"Did your father get a nap today?"

The boy shrugged. "I don't know. Maybe."

Beth tried to shake the fear that settled around her like a misty shroud.

"Something wrong, Miss Ryken?"

Beth gave the boy a bright smile. It wasn't right to make the boy nervous with her worries. "No. Why?"

He looked her straight in the eye. "Do you like my dad?"

Beth's smile faltered and fell. What exactly was Corey asking? "Of course I like your dad. He's a nice man."

"Yeah." Corey focused back on the game. There couldn't be any hidden meaning behind his question. He was only seven years old.

Beth settled on the couch and Peanut made a wobbly jump into her lap. The dog stretched and then nuzzled her hand for pats. She stroked the dog's fur and puzzled over Corey's question. The kid wasn't looking to play matchmaker, was he?

"Corey, why did you ask me if I liked your dad?"

He shrugged. "Just wondered."

"Oh." See? Nothing.

Beth was paranoid, or maybe everyone saw through her to the truth. She liked Nick, all right. She liked him a lot. Maybe too much.

* * *

Nick stepped into Mary Ryken's warm kitchen the next morning. Sunlight streamed through the windows and the smell of sausage made his belly rumble. Corey's painting had been framed and it now hung in a place of honor on the kitchen wall. It looked good there. It looked even more cheerful as sunlight shined off the glass. A promise of better days to come?

He shook his head at such sleepy imaginings. He'd had an eventful Saturday night on patrol. He'd checked on a noisy party with a guy passed out on the ground by his car, and then he'd been called to a domestic dispute within a town smaller than LeNaro.

Domestic violence calls were the ones he hated most. They were unpredictable and scary. But not last night. The couple had made up by the time he'd arrived. They'd been verbally but not physically abusive, so all had ended well with promises of keeping it toned down in future. Nick had filled out his reports during downtime before dawn.

"Morning, Nick." Mary Ryken stood by the stove wearing a ruffled apron and flipping pancakes.

He yawned. "Sorry."

Beth peered at him with concern. "You look tired."

And you look beautiful. He didn't dare say it, but

he didn't look away from her, either. Her hair was tousled from sleep and it was all Nick could do not to yank her into his arms. "I'm okay."

Silence settled in the kitchen.

Nick jerked back to the present when he realized no one was talking or paying attention to the small TV droning in the background. He glanced at his son, who wore a curious expression. Mary, too, had been watching them, a pancake poised on her plastic turner. Even the dog sat with her ears perked high as if waiting for something. Probably a scrap of food to fall.

Nick glanced back at Beth, who hunted for something in the fridge. She seemed so perfect in every way. Even cheerful in the morning. But Nick needed a bigger sign than his mushy heart beating too fast before he considered Beth Ryken right for them.

Right for him.

"Why don't you let us keep Corey for church and then Beth can run him home later. That way you can get some sleep."

"No...." Hadn't these two women done enough for him?

"It's no problem," Beth said. "I'll bring him home after lunch."

Nick looked at Corey. "That work for you, bud?"

"Yup." His son dug into a small stack of pancakes with a smile. The kid liked it here. Why shouldn't he?

Mary touched Nick's shoulder as she handed him a plate of pancakes and sausage. "Sit down and eat, and then go."

"Thanks." Nick meant it.

He couldn't begin to express his gratitude to these two women, and even the dog. Corey flourished here. And that liveliness transferred when they went home, too. Especially since the arrival of Peanut. His boy was healing.

He slipped into a chair next to Beth. She didn't have a plate of food, only an empty mug. "Aren't you eating?"

She got up fast. "More coffee first. Can I get you a cup?"

He shook his head as he jammed a forkful of fluffy pancakes into his mouth. "Milk?"

She laughed at his muffled request.

He watched Beth move around the kitchen as if trying to keep busy. When she set a glass of milk in front of him, he smiled and nodded.

She didn't sit back down. Instead she leaned against the sink and drank her coffee.

He cleaned his plate in no time, but no matter how much he ate, a stronger hunger had settled over him. It felt right. *This* felt right. He and his son and Beth in the kitchen having breakfast together.

It didn't matter that they were in her mother's house. It felt as if they were a family.

"More?" Mary had another stack of pancakes ready.

"Please." He lifted his plate. Tired to the bone but not ready to leave. Not yet.

He glanced at Beth and noticed that she looked pale. Worn, even, as though she hadn't slept well. The light smudges under her eyes were barely visible, but they were there. Had Corey or the dog kept her up? He was used to getting up once a night with Peanut to let her outside, but he fell back to sleep easily enough that it didn't bother him.

"How many times did you have to get up with the dog?" he asked.

Beth shifted. "Only once."

"And Corey?"

"I didn't wake up at all," Corey said.

Nick glanced at Beth and Mary, who confirmed it with nods of agreement. "I didn't hear a thing." Mary finally sat down to eat.

"Good. I'll take off, then. I can take Peanut with me."

"I'll bring her," Beth said with a wave of dismissal. But she wouldn't look at him. "Go home and sleep."

Nick nodded. Funny, but he felt as if he was already home. He looked at the dog they'd had for nearly a week now with no claims made on her. She slept with Corey, and Nick hadn't heard a peep out of the boy ever since. His son used to stir and get up a couple of times during the night. On occasion, Corey had called out for his mom before drifting back to sleep. Those nights had torn Nick in two.

He ruffled his son's hair. "See you later, bud."

His son smiled up at him. "Bye, Dad."

His heart full, Nick glanced at Beth. "You're going to need directions to my house."

"You're right. Let me get some paper and a pen." She hurried into the dining room like a flash of light. What was wrong with her?

He followed her.

She snatched what she needed and turned quick, almost running into his chest, and wobbled.

He steadied her by gently grabbing her shoulders. "You okay?"

"Yeah, why?" She sounded breathless. Agitated.

"I don't know. You seem...different." He slid his hands down her arms before letting them drop away from her. Before he pulled her close.

She cleared her throat. "Nope. I'm fine."

He narrowed his eyes but didn't press her. "Okay."

"Here, draw me a map." She handed him the paper and pen and backed away a few steps, absently rubbing her arms.

He looked at her closely, giving her a chance to tell him what was wrong.

"Directions?" She pointed to the paper.

He leaned over the dining room table and drew. Then he wrote down his address. She already had his cell phone number. "It's not far."

"Oh. I know where you live. I didn't recognize the street address, is all." Beth looked like her normal self again.

Nick wanted to shake his head. Women were a mystery he'd never solve. "Have you thought about how I can even up the score?"

Her pretty blue eyes clouded over with confusion.

"I owe you big-time, remember?"

She smiled. A big, bright and beautiful smile. "Oh, I'm thinking."

"Make it good."

Her eyes widened, and then she looked worried all over again. "I'll try."

Chapter Eight

Later that afternoon, Beth drove a few miles out of town with her windows down. It was hot for the first week of May and that probably boded well for a warm summer. Nick didn't live far from the northern lake of Lake Leelanau. She spotted a public-beach sign and smiled. North Lake had the best sandy beaches.

Beth loved the beach. Any beach. She had plenty to choose from, too. Living on the Leelanau Peninsula, which was surrounded by Lake Michigan and split in the middle by Lake Leelanau, Beth took advantage of the water every chance she could. Give her sun, sand and a book and she was a happy camper. She hoped Corey would enjoy those things, too, especially books.

Beth glanced at the boy buckled into a booster seat that her mom had purchased before Nick could intervene. Her mother had given Nick a lecture on the ease of keeping a seat at their house and wouldn't hear another word about it.

It wouldn't be long before Corey turned eight and wouldn't need a booster seat. It wouldn't be long before the school year ended and Corey wouldn't need her, either. The thought of not seeing the boy every day brought a sharp squeeze deep in her chest.

She'd lost her teacher mode for sure. And maybe Diane had been more concerned about her and how much it would hurt if she got too close to this little boy who'd stolen her heart from the get-go.

Too close to his father, who'd done the same thing.

"Looks like we're here," Beth said.

Peanut lay in Corey's lap, but her ears perked up when they pulled into the driveway. Did the dog know they were home? Her new home?

"This is it, right?"

"Yup." Corey got out and set Peanut on the grass. They both trotted toward the front deck.

Beth looked around. The yard was vast with mature oak trees lending shade to the south end of the house. And what a cute house! Nick had bought a ranch with a peaked roof addition on the front that gave the place a cape-cottage look. Tan with white shutters and an ornamental white picket fence in the front, it was somewhere she could easily see herself.

This was what Beth wanted, only she didn't want to share it with a man in law enforcement. She let out a sigh and walked toward the house.

Nick came out of the garage wearing khaki shorts and a faded T-shirt. His face and arms shone with sweat. The stubble along his jaw looked pretty good, too. "Hey. Wow, is it that time already?"

Beth nodded. "What are you up to?"

"Putting in a fence for the dog."

"You were supposed to sleep." The breeze played with her hair, so Beth anchored it behind her ears.

"I did. For a bit." He gestured for her to follow him. "Come on, I'll show you."

Corey and Peanut must have gone inside, because they were nowhere in sight. Beth walked behind Nick into the backyard, which seemed to go on forever. "How much land do you have?"

"Couple acres. I own to the edge of those woods."

He'd been putting in welded wire fence anchored by wooden posts. By the looks of the posts sticking out of the ground, he planned on fencing in a good-sized area, too.

"It works for now. Eventually, I'll get picket fencing for the whole backyard, but with the puppies, I'm worried they might slip right through the slats."

Beth's heart melted even more. Nick Grey was pure mush. "You're doing this for the puppies?"

"And Peanut. No one's claimed her, so she's ours. She'll need a safe place to run around outside."

"Can I help?"

Nick gave her a shocked look. "You're kidding, right?"

"I wouldn't offer if I didn't want to."

He narrowed his gaze as he took in her striped capris and white T-shirt. "You'll get dirty."

Beth laughed. Did he think she was afraid of a little dirt? "So? I wash well."

He gave her that lopsided grin that made her stomach flip. "You smell good, too."

"We'll see about that after we're done."

Nick gave her a nod. "Thanks."

"You're welcome." Beth rationalized her offer to help. The dog and the forthcoming puppies made as good an excuse as any, but she knew better.

She wanted to stick around and help Nick because it meant spending time with him. And that brought her closer and closer to breaking the vow she'd made not to date cops.

"Come on inside. I'll show you the house before we get started. Is your mom expecting you back?"

"No."

Beth's mom had practically tossed her out the door with orders to take her time. Obviously, her mother already liked Nick and had no qualms about what he did for a living.

They stepped into the house from the back deck.

A huge kitchen done in white cupboards and pale blue walls with a dining area greeted them. Beth found herself smiling again. "Nice. This is really nice."

He looked at her. "All I need to do is fill it."

Surely he meant with furniture. The place was pretty bare. No knickknacks or artwork on the walls. A table with chairs in the dining room, louvered blinds instead of curtains gracing the windows. In the living room, Nick had a recliner with a floor lamp beside it, a TV and a coffee table in front of a sofa. On that sofa a little boy lay curled up around a pregnant dog. Both were sleeping.

Nick stopped and stared a moment, his eyes softening at the sight of his son. "Why's he wiped out?"

Beth hoped Nick didn't mind. "We stayed up sort of late watching a Disney movie last night. And then Mom made a small turkey for lunch. Which reminds me, I have leftovers for you. They're in a cooler in my car."

Nick shook his head. "She doesn't have to do that."

"Trust me, you're doing her a favor. She loves to cook."

Her mom had taken the Grey boys under her wing. Cooking was something Mary Ryken enjoyed, and making sure Nick and Corey ate well gave her mom purpose. Or maybe it was feeling needed that seemed to stave off her mother's shopping sprees. Would that change come summer when Nick found other arrangements for Corey?

Beth could volunteer to watch him, but that wasn't a good idea. Spending the summer with Corey meant slipping right into a mom role. Beth wouldn't mind a bit, but how fair could it be to act like a mother to Corey if she wouldn't accept his father?

"Want to see the rest of the house?"

"Of course. Lead the way." Beth followed him.

Nice finished basement. Nice bedroom for Corey, bathroom, and then finally, they ended up in Nick's room. It was a large bedroom with a sliding glass door that opened onto the back deck. Okay. She officially loved his house. "Nice."

"I think so." He foraged through a dresser drawer and then tossed a dark blue T-shirt at her. "Here. You can wear this while we work. Do you want a pair of jeans or shorts?"

Beth clutched his T-shirt and raised her eyebrow. "Your shorts won't fit me."

He cocked his head and studied her hips. "Sure they will. Might be baggy around your waist, though."

She felt her cheeks heat. He was crazy but sweet. And his comments made her feel small and feminine. "The shirt is fine. I'll be a minute."

Beth dashed for the bathroom to change her top. A splash of cold water might be in order, too.

It didn't take long before Beth met him in the kitchen wearing his shirt. It hung on her shoulders. Her cheeks were still rosy. She was the most beautiful and caring woman he'd ever met.

"What?"

He shook his head. "Nothing. Would you like some lemonade?"

"Please." She looked away.

He poured, wondering what they were doing dancing around each other this way. He handed her a glass and noticed her feet. They were pretty, too, and in flip-flops. "Those won't do."

"Huh?"

"I'll get you a pair of work boots and socks."

A nervous-sounding giggle slipped out of her. "Okay."

Back in his bedroom, he retrieved the protective footwear. Passing the bathroom, he noticed her pristine white T-shirt folded and draped over the towel rack. The sight stopped him cold.

The fierce longing for the right woman to share in raising Corey cut him in two. But Beth didn't want to get involved with a cop, and he shouldn't get involved with anyone right now. Right?

That conviction didn't ring true anymore. Not with the attachment Corey had for Beth.

He returned to the kitchen and spotted Beth peering out of the sliding glass door. "Boots might be big, but they'll keep you safe from injury."

She turned and smiled. "Thanks."

"No, thank you for your help. It'll go much faster with two of us."

She opened her mouth and then closed it. Something was definitely on her mind.

Nick's gut tensed. He hoped it wasn't about Corey. "What?"

Beth bit her bottom lip and then cleared her throat. "I have a favor to ask you."

"Name it. I owe you big-time, remember?"

"This is big."

He stepped closer, looking forward to what she might ask of him. "It should be."

"Will you go with me to a wedding I'm in Saturday?"

He blinked. "That's it?"

"Guys hate weddings, or so I'm told."

Wearing a suit and tie, making small talk with people he didn't know and would probably never see again—yup, weddings were a drag. "You're in it?"

"A bridesmaid for my friend Eva. You met her and her fiancé at the pizza place."

Even worse. He'd end up standing around and waiting. Why was there so much waiting around with weddings? But dancing might be involved.

With Beth. Nick wasn't opposed to that. He suspected holding her close would be worth it.

"Sure. I'll go."

She smiled. "Great. I thought Corey could come, too, since the whole thing is outside in a cherry orchard. My mom will be there, so she can help keep an eye on him. It'd be a great chance for you to meet some people in the community."

Nick chuckled. Dancing didn't sound promising in an afternoon garden wedding. It might be boring, too. "You don't have to sell me on it. I said I'd go."

"Right." Beth took the boots and socks from him and then sat down to put them on. Her cheeks blazed.

"What time?" This wasn't a date. Far from it. But then, if it was a garden-party thing, what did she need him for?

"The wedding's at six in the evening. You can meet me there. Maybe pick up my mom? She knows where to go."

"This is an outside wedding at night?" In May. In Northern Michigan.

Beth had laced up each boot. They were too big. Along with the baggy T-shirt, she looked as if she'd been caught playing dress-up in her father's closet. "In their cherry orchard that'll be in full bloom. It's quite a sight to see, too. Don't worry, there will be tents set up for dinner and the band. But it's not supposed to rain according to the forecast."

Even though he'd lived up north for a short time, he knew forecasts changed on a dime. There was a saying he'd heard in the department: *if you don't like the weather, just wait, it'll change.*

Anything could change in less than a week. Including his resolve to wait until he knew Beth better before asking her out. A band meant dancing, and he really liked the sound of that.

"I'll be there."

"Thank you." Beth smiled, looking relieved.

He smiled back. "Let's wrestle the fence."

"Okay." She peeked into the living room to check on Corey. "He's still asleep."

"Maybe we can get this done before he wakes up. With you helping, it shouldn't take too long since the posts are in." Nick handed Beth a pair of work gloves.

She took them without a word and followed him outside.

"I need you to pull the length of fence tight against the posts so I can hammer staples in and attach it. Sound good?"

Beth nodded. "Good."

They worked in silence at first. Together they'd unravel the length of twelve-gauge wire fencing and straighten it. Beth held it firm while he hammered it in place. She was strong and capable even clomping around in his oversize boots. They worked well as a team, nailing one post after another. She moved with him and didn't flinch when he brushed against her.

"Thanks for doing this." He slammed a staple in place.

"No problem. Glad to do it."

Nick sat back on his haunches and looked up at her. She'd pulled her hair back into a messy ponytail. "That's what amazes me."

She wrinkled her nose. "This? No biggie."

"My wife would never have done this."

"No?"

He shook his head. "No."

"What happened?"

"To her? Or to us?" Nick couldn't believe he was going there.

"Both," Beth whispered.

They unrolled the next length of fence. "She was killed in a car accident, but our marriage was a wreck long before that."

Beth's gaze flew to his. "I'm sorry."

"Yeah, me, too. I rushed into it without really knowing her." He stopped rolling fence. "Remember what I told you about Susan breaking the plates?"

Beth nodded. "Yeah."

"Looking back, I wonder if there wasn't more I could have done to help her cope. Things had really deteriorated that last year. Frustration had grown into resentment." He blew out his breath. "Maybe if I'd been around more at night, I could have seen what was happening to her. Made her get help. I don't know."

Beth laid her gloved hand on his. "Didn't her folks notice anything?"

"Her mom said it was anxiety and stress. Susan worked part-time while Corey was at school. I don't know where the stress came from, unless it all came from me."

He'd been working an undercover case he couldn't walk away from. Not then. He'd planned on going to a day shift, but the case had dragged on, and then Susan was killed.

He glanced back at Beth. "Sorry to unload."

Her eyes shone with compassion, and she gave him a bright smile. "Don't be. We're friends, right?"

"Right." She was naive to think so. He didn't know what they were.

"Hey, Dad, can Peanut come out?" Corey stood on the back deck rubbing his eyes.

"Sure, son." Nick glanced at their fence. Only two posts left to go to finish enclosing the backyard. He'd have to build a gate somewhere, but he'd figure that out later. "Keep an eye on her while we finish up."

"Okay." Corey ran in the backyard with Peanut at his heels. She moved pretty fast for a pregnant dog.

"He's settling in here, isn't he?" Beth's voice was quiet as they pulled the fence tight on the last post.

"I think so. Having the dog really helps. And you." Nick checked his watch. "You want to stick around for dinner and then do some reading together with Corey?"

"Sure." She handed him her work gloves. "I'll go wash up."

Nick watched her walk up the steps of his back deck. She slipped out of his work boots and socks and then disappeared into the house. It felt right having her here.

"Is Miss Ryken staying for dinner?" Corey was by his side.

"That okay with you?" Nick looked down at his son. Seemed silly to call her Miss Ryken now that they'd become friends. But he'd rather wait until the school year was over before he gave his son permission to call her by her first name. Maybe Miss Beth would do come summer.

Corey grinned. "Yup."

He ruffled the boy's hair, which was in need of a trim. "Come on. Let's wash up, too."

Stepping inside, Nick knew they'd become far more than friends. They'd become a family.

Beth cleared the dishes from the table to load them into the dishwasher. Nick had grilled hamburgers for dinner and Beth had made a salad. Her mother's leftovers had been tucked into his sparsely filled fridge for another day. The guy didn't stock up much. Good thing her mom had sent leftovers.

"Last one." Nick set the greasy burger plate on the counter and then leaned close and sniffed her neck.

Beth turned. "What are you doing?"

"You still smell nice."

She wielded a butter knife. "Watch it, mister."

He cocked his eyebrow in challenge.

"Don't think I won't use it," she warned.

He laughed at her mock fierceness. "You wouldn't hurt a fly."

"My father taught me self-defense moves when I was a kid." She'd had to use it years ago to help Eva get away from her bully of a then-boyfriend.

"Care to see if they work?" Nick teased her.

She wasn't biting on his line. "I know they work."

"I used to teach a self-defense class to my fellow undercover officers. Several were women."

She touched his nose. "Is that how you got this broken? Did those women gang up on you?"

He glanced at the dining room table, but Corey had already gone into the living room.

Beth could hear the TV.

"A different gang and the odds weren't in my favor."

Beth felt her eyes widen as the reality of his

work came crashing in, obliterating their easy flirtation. "That's why I don't date cops."

"Because they get their noses broken?"

She poked him in the ribs to move so she could load up the dishwasher. "No. It's how they get broken that bothers me."

He reached for a plate that she'd rinsed and settled it into the rack. "That was when I worked undercover. I had to play rough-and-tumble to prove I was a punk. No big deal."

Beth couldn't imagine what Nick might have had to do in the name of justice. She didn't want to know. She hated the thought of him getting beat up, or worse. The way he'd sloughed it off as nothing silenced her pretty good. They filled the rest of the dishwasher without another word.

When they were done, Nick turned it on. "I'm not reckless, Beth."

She glanced at him. The hum of the dishwasher spraying water nearly drowned out his softly spoken words, but she'd heard them loud and clear. He was making his case. "My father wasn't, either."

"Life has risks. Some occupations hold more than others, but you shouldn't stop living because of fear."

She narrowed her gaze.

She lived. Didn't she? *Yeah, right.* As Eva's roommate and now her mom's, what did that say about her ability to step out and take risks? She saved her pennies for what? A rainy day?

"I can choose what risks to embrace."

"But what if you miss out on something God has for you?" Nick didn't look as confident as his words sounded. Was he trying to say that they might be meant for each other?

She refused to put herself through the same pain of her father's death. This afternoon Nick had confessed to some of what he'd been through with his late wife. How much had stemmed from what he did for a living? The life of a cop's wife was filled with worry. And fear. How did a woman let go of that?

Beth didn't have to, and that was the point. She had a choice here. "Let's work on Corey's reading homework before I leave. It's getting late."

Too late to rescind her request for Nick to accompany her to Eva's wedding. She'd asked him out of pure selfishness. She didn't want to be standing on the sidelines waiting for sympathy dance requests from Eva's brothers. She didn't want to dance with men she'd tower over, either.

But the real reason she'd asked was because she didn't want to show up to such a romantic affair alone.

Nick was a lot like wedding cake. Harmless in small chunks, but too much and she'd be hurting. She made a mental promise to take him in moderation until her stopping point at the end of the school year.

"All right. We can settle around the table." Nick cleared off the salt and pepper shakers.

"I have a better idea. Let's write haiku in the living room and make a game of it."

"High-what?" Nick gave her a funny look.

Beth laughed. "Come on, and I'll show you."

They gathered around the coffee table and Beth handed out a couple of sheets of notepaper while Nick clicked off the TV.

"What are we doing?" Corey slipped down beside her.

"A game."

Corey looked at his dad. "This doesn't look like a game."

Nick chuckled. "Don't worry, bud, I don't know how to do this, either."

Beth smiled. "We're going to write a poem called a haiku."

Corey groaned.

"Haiku are fun poems and they don't have to rhyme," Beth explained. "Five syllables or beats, then seven, then back to five. Here…I'll do one so you can see what I mean."

She scribbled down a few lines and read it back using her fingers to show the number of beats in each line. "Peanut is pregnant. Her puppies will arrive soon. What will we name them?"

"Let me see that." Nick pulled the paper closer and counted, then stared at her. "How'd you do that so fast?"

Beth grinned and looked at Corey. "Practice. I love these things. Corey, do you want to give it a go?"

The boy shrugged.

"We'll help you. Let's start with a topic. How about baseball?"

Corey looked lost.

Beth gave him an encouraging nod. "How about this.... The Tigers are great."

"They like to grill big fat steaks," Nick added.

Corey giggled.

And Beth nodded. "I think you've got it. We need a last line, though, five beats."

"And throw the ball...far?" Corey counted each sound on his fingers.

Beth whooped. "Yes! That's it! Corey, you're good."

Nick gave his son a high five and then smiled at her with admiration. "Let's do more."

Beth nodded.

Nick and Corey both waited for her to give more clues, but her throat suddenly felt tight. This had really worked. Corey looked excited to continue, and Nick? She didn't want to think about how wonderful Nick looked. Or how spending a Sunday together made it feel as if they were a family.

Because thinking along those lines forced her to face the fact that she'd have to make a choice and soon. Follow her head or follow her heart.

No matter which one she followed, someone was bound to get hurt. Eventually.

Chapter Nine

"Beth, Mr. Grey, thanks for meeting with me." Diane sat back down at her desk.

"Of course." Beth was used to this sort of thing.

She and Diane had met with the parents of at-risk kids before. Sometimes the parents were willing, sometimes they weren't. But this was weird because she knew Nick pretty well.

And cared for him, too.

"No problem." Nick wore his deputy sheriff's uniform. At least he'd left his hat in the car so he didn't look quite so formidable. "What's this about? Beth said we'd discuss how Corey has been settling in, but there's more, isn't there?"

Diane nodded. "A little. Yes. Corey's previous school had some troubling notations—"

Nick snorted contempt. "They labeled him without understanding what he'd been through."

Beth held her tongue. And her hands neatly in

her lap. She'd nearly reached out to Nick at the strain in his voice. But that wouldn't be good, not in front of Diane. The counselor had seen them out together, and Nick had called her by her first name.

Diane didn't falter. "He's showing improvement. He's socializing, making friends, and his reading is progressing."

"Then you won't recommend he be held back, right?" Nick had moved forward in his seat.

Diane looked at her for help.

"We don't make those recommendations until closer to the end of the year," Beth said.

Nick's eyes narrowed. "How close?"

"The last couple of weeks."

"Miss Ryken knows I won't agree to hold my son back."

Diane nodded. "Yes, she told me that. Look, Mr. Grey, if Beth believes it's best for Corey, and he scores well for repeating second grade, you'll need to sign a waiver that you're refusing retention. Those forms follow Corey until he graduates."

Nick nodded. "Understood. But he's doing better."

"I'd say." Diane leaned back in her chair. "Thanks to both of you working together instead of in opposition."

Nick looked surprised.

Beth was, too. Where was Diane going with this?

"The first time I met with Corey, he said that he wanted a family. A new family that would never leave."

Beth's belly tumbled. Diane hadn't told her that. That whole teacher-mode warning made sense now.

Nick puffed out his cheeks, then released his breath in a whoosh. "He feels abandoned after I had him live with his grandparents."

Diane looked even more serious. "Not now, he doesn't. Whatever it is that you two are doing outside of schoolwork and tutoring, keep it up. Corey is settling in nicely because he has both his teacher's and his father's support. Inside the classroom and out of it. But if you're dating, that will play right into Corey's new-family fantasy."

Beth glanced at Nick. "We're not dating."

He looked determined. "Not yet."

Diane looked between the two of them. "Whatever you decide to do, keep in mind that the outcome of your relationship will have an impact on Corey. Now, let's go over Corey's progress in detail."

Beth cringed. She knew what Diane said without really saying it. Getting romantically involved with Nick had to be a one-way street. Go all the way or don't go at all. Marriage or maintain friendship. From Corey's perspective, a breakup would be a form of abandonment. Another loss and possible setback. But if they were to remain friends until Corey was truly settled, would that make a positive difference?

Diane went over the transcripts from Corey's old school and compared those sparse notes to where he was now. Beth kept progress logs on all her students. She had to. Part of her job was comparing those with the other second-grade class. She and Julie worked as a team to ensure everyone met their benchmarks. Nick listened, but his expression grew darker the more they went over Corey's transcripts from his old school. "I never realized it had been that bad."

Diane shrugged. "The information is incomplete. And contradictory."

Beth remembered reading one teacher's notes that Corey had cried a lot. He'd isolate himself from the other students and cry. And like most kids that age who had no idea how to help, they left him alone. And Nick had been gone, too.

Beth's heart bled for the little guy who'd felt all alone. Corey wanted a family. But he had one. He had grandparents and a good father. What else was he after?

A mom.

Of course he was. Poor kid. But Beth wasn't sure she could fill that role. Not if it meant becoming the wife of a cop.

After their meeting, Beth turned to Nick in the hallway of the administration office. "Are you ready to pick up Corey at my mom's or do you have to return to work?

"I'm done for the day. I'll walk you over."

Beth agreed.

Slipping outside into late-May sunshine, Nick stalled her with a touch. "You're not going to suggest holding Corey back, after all those good things your school counselor had to say?"

Beth had to make him understand so many things. "It's not solely a matter of opinion. We look for certain criteria and aptitude when completing the required paperwork that recommends retention. Scoring helps narrow that decision."

He shook his head. "Corey's a smart kid. He's going to catch up."

Beth hoped so. "And we've got to remain a team in agreement on our friendship. No dating, Nick."

He nodded but didn't look convinced.

"Are you going to talk to my class for Jobs Day?" Corey bounced on the bed. "Thomas's dad is a chef and he's going to be there."

"Uh-huh." Nick attempted to tie his tie for the third time. "We'll see, bud."

"Miss Ryken said it was okay, didn't she?" Corey threw himself in the middle of the bed once again.

"Yes, she did." Nick had been formally invited to speak for Occupation Day in Beth's class.

He wasn't thrilled about it, but he'd do it because

Corey wanted him to. He'd do anything to help Beth and that school counselor pull for Corey to pass second grade. Staying involved helped with that. His son's old school had passed unfair judgment on Corey because Susan's parents had gone to all the parent-teacher meetings at school. That hadn't done his boy any favors.

So he'd talk to Beth's class to prove he was involved. He cared. But kids loved all the gore of excitement-filled stories. Those kind of tales would only reinforce Beth's fears and maybe scare his son. He'd keep it tame. Thankfully, that wasn't hard to do since moving here.

He looked through the mirror at his son. "And stop jumping on my bed. You'll wrinkle your suit."

Corey pulled at his tie as he slipped to the floor. "Why do I have to wear this, anyway?"

Nick smiled. "Because it's a wedding."

"So?"

"So we're supposed to look nice at weddings."

"Stupid wedding. Do I have to go?"

Nick chuckled. Corey had wanted to go before he knew about wearing a suit. Maybe Nick should have arranged for Corey to go to Thomas's house instead. Too late now. "Yes, you do. We're picking up Mrs. Ryken on the way."

Corey smiled. "Does Mary have to wear a suit?"

"No, bud. She's probably going to wear a dress." Nick still didn't like it that Beth's mom had given his boy permission to call her by her first name. But Mary liked it that way. Who was he to refuse the woman's wish?

Nick stepped back, finally satisfied that his tie was straight. He hadn't worn a suit in ages. Susan's funeral might have been the last time. A day he'd rather not remember. Corey had been devastated. Lost.

He glanced at the boy. His son had come back to life. He read, too. Brokenly still, but better than before. The haiku poetry game Beth had taught them Sunday night had been a huge hit with Corey. Every night this week, they spent time making up different haiku and laughing at their results.

Nick had framed the first poem Corey wrote on paper with Beth's help. It had cracked them all up and Nick cherished the memory of seeing his boy laugh so hard. It'd been a long time, and Nick didn't want to forget that moment. A milestone.

He glanced at the framed piece of paper displayed on his bedroom wall.

I like scary bugs
Icky, yucky, crawly, splat
Hairy legs and eyes

Nick smiled. He owed Beth a whole lot more than attending a wedding with her. He owed her his patience. *Friendship,* she'd said. That was getting increasingly difficult to maintain.

"Ready, Dad?"

He looked down at his son with his freshly cut red hair. Nick had gotten a trim, too. A Saturday morning spent at the barbershop in town as father and son. Then they went out for breakfast. Corey had read the menu and chose pancakes. They'd come a long way.

"I'm ready."

After letting Peanut inside from a potty run, they left through the garage and climbed into his SUV. It didn't take long to reach town. When they'd pulled into Mary Ryken's driveway, Nick got out and headed for the house.

Mary met him on the porch. An attractive woman in her fifties, she wore a yellow dress that fluttered when she walked. "How nice you look, Nick."

"Thanks. You, too." Nick held open the passenger-side door for Beth's mom.

He was perplexed that Mary hadn't remarried. Had she even dated in the twelve years since her husband's death? If she had, would Beth still have held on to the fear from her dad's death? Maybe Beth would have accepted him if she'd finished growing up with a stepfather who'd taken away the sting of her loss.

At Corey's tender age, he needed another mom,

wanted another mom, but she had to be the right woman. A woman like Beth. According to the school counselor, they shouldn't jump into anything until they were sure. Nick agreed.

"Oh, Corey, you look very handsome."

Nick gave his son a pointed look through the rearview mirror.

Corey straightened up from slouching in his booster seat. "Thanks, Mary."

"You're welcome." Mary fussed with her dress before buckling up. "You're going to drive out of town and then head north on Eagle Highway. Marsh Orchards is only a few miles out."

Nick nodded. He had an idea where they were going. In the month he'd been patrolling the county, he'd come to know the area pretty well. Leelanau County was filled with cherry orchards and vineyards. A safe area, too, all things considered.

Would he ever convince Beth of that?

By the time they pulled into the long driveway that led to Marsh Orchards, Nick was taken by the beauty of the place. A cherry-red farmhouse sat on a hilly mound with good views. Following the signs, Nick parked, got out and stared at the vista before him. Beth had been right. The orchard was something to see. The cherry trees were heavy with white blossoms, and petals fluttered to the ground like falling snow. Fat and soft.

"Come on. We'll sit on the bride's side." Mary bustled forward.

Nick followed with his hand tight around Corey's. He didn't need the boy running off somewhere. Especially after they spotted a couple of kids close to Corey's age darting around the cherry trees. The sun hung in the western sky, but it was a good three hours from setting and still shone with warmth. Another benefit to moving so far north, the days were even longer, especially as summer approached. And this was one beautiful spring day.

They sat down in white folding chairs as a woman with a harp began playing typical wedding music. It was light and airy sounding, and Nick felt as if he'd walked into one of Corey's books. If a giant white rabbit showed up, he'd worry.

Chuckling at his thoughts, he spotted the tent Beth had mentioned. It was a huge white wedding variety with roll-down walls positioned on high ground beyond a pole barn. Inside he glimpsed tall propane heaters to ward off the night chill. Should be an interesting evening.

A hush settled among the guests and the music changed tempo. Nick felt a tug on his sleeve and looked down. "Yeah, bud?"

"What happens now?"

Nick smiled. "The bride will come out and meet her groom."

"Who are they?" Corey pointed at the men who

had taken their places in front near a flowered arch. Two of them Nick remembered from the pizza shop. Adam and Ryan. The third man standing was older and bald. And the minister looked like a lighter version of Ryan. Brother, maybe?

"That's the groom and his friends. The groom is the one getting married today."

Corey nodded.

The music changed again and everyone stood.

Corey, on tiptoe, craned his neck to peer around the adults who watched the bride come down the steps of the house. "There's Miss Ryken."

"Doesn't she look beautiful?" Mary cooed.

"Yeah." Nick wasn't sure if she meant the bride or her daughter. Didn't matter. Beth looked amazing.

Beth and another bridesmaid lifted the back of the bride's dress, keeping it from snagging on the gravel of the driveway. Once they reached grass, the women fluffed the bride's dress and then slipped into single file in front of her. A dark-haired woman and then Beth.

The pink dress Beth wore accentuated every fine curve and long length of her. Her hair had been bundled on top of her head, giving her even more height. Walking between the two petite women, Beth stood regal. Gorgeous.

Once the women were standing in place, Beth looked his way.

Nick smiled.

She smiled back.

Nick drank in the sight of her. From a distance it was easy to do without being caught. But then Beth glanced his way a couple times and each time, he smiled instead of looking away. She nearly forgot to take the bride's bouquet so the couple could exchange rings.

Enough staring. Beth had a job to do.

Thankfully, the ceremony was brief. Corey's fidgets weren't too bad. The kid asked only twice what they were doing and why. Finally, the bride and groom kissed to seal the deal as a married couple.

Nick felt another tug on his sleeve. "Yeah, bud?"

"Will you marry Miss Ryken?"

It was a rare occurrence for Nick to be struck speechless. He might not use a whole lot of words, but he'd always found a few when he needed them.

Not now, though. "Uh…"

"She could be my new mom," Corey added as if trying to convince him to agree.

Nick didn't need to be convinced. He glanced at Mary, who hid a smirk behind a tissue. He'd get no help there.

He faced his son, who waited for an answer. "I don't know, bud. We'll talk about that later."

"Okay." Corey shrugged, not realizing the bomb

he'd just thrown had confirmed everything the school counselor had said.

Nick felt the shrapnel like pinpricks all over his skin as that question reverberated through his brain. Hadn't he thought along those same lines? But he couldn't rush. For Corey's sake, he had to be sure. And he had to be sure she'd say yes.

After the ceremony and another round of pictures, Beth slipped into a seat at the table for four with her mom, Corey and Nick. Shame on him for staring during the service. Shame on her for staring back.

"Hey."

Nick looked surprised. "No wedding-party table?"

"Nope. The bride and groom have their own, so the rest of us can mingle." She chose a couple hors d'oeuvres offered by a waiter.

"Nice."

Beth gulped her water. Something about the way Nick looked at her made her feel warm all over. Nervous, even.

"You look pretty," Corey said around a mouthful of dried cherries and chocolate. Small dishes of the stuff graced every table.

"Thank you, Corey." She didn't dare look at Nick. Beth had read the appreciation in his gaze several times. She didn't need his words, didn't want them, either. And certainly not in front of her mother.

After a brief silence while Nick and Corey pounded down the snacks and cherry mix, Beth breathed a little easier. Nick didn't say anything about the way she looked.

"Lovely wedding." Her mother fluffed the brand-new dress she wore.

"It is."

Her mother had ordered the yellow confection from an online store before Beth could intervene. One more frilly dress headed for the back of her mother's closet after tonight, never to be worn again. Beth supposed only one extravagant purchase wasn't too bad considering her mom had a habit of ordering a few to try on and choose from. Her mom was trying to curb her spending habits and making some progress.

"So what's next?" Nick asked.

"Dinner and then the band will set up and emcee the rest of the usual wedding stuff." Beth had been given the reception plan by Eva months ago. They'd cut the cake and throw the bouquet and garter all in between an evening of dancing.

"Good. The sound of that harp is getting old."

"I agree." Beth laughed.

Being sandwiched between two tiny women in pictures had been bad enough, but tromping around in a short pink sheath of silk with harp music playing in the background made her feel like a giant. An underdressed one, at that.

Dinner was barely served when the tinkling of glasses started. The bride and groom had only just sat down.

"What's that for?" Corey's eyes went wide.

The crowd cheered as Adam and Eva shared a quick kiss.

Beth glanced at Nick, and he nodded for her to go ahead and explain. "At weddings people tap their glasses so the bride and groom will kiss."

Corey made a face. "Why?"

Beth gestured that it was Nick's turn this time.

"I don't know, bud. Maybe because kissing is fun."

"Ewww."

They all laughed, but Beth caught Nick looking at her again.

"Trust me. You'll think so one day."

Corey stuck out his tongue and clutched at his throat, playing dead. "No way."

Relieved by the arrival of food, Beth heard her stomach growl. She was hungry, all right, having skipped lunch, but anticipation for the evening ahead gnawed at her. She almost couldn't eat. Almost.

Glancing sideways at Nick, so handsome in his navy suit, Beth could hardly wait to feel his arms around her. Not exactly smart thinking for a woman who didn't want to date a cop, but tonight she intended to put all that aside and enjoy the dance floor.

A Scripture from First Corinthians flashed through her mind, reminding her that all things were lawful but not all things were profitable. Or wise. Could she dance close to Nick and still stay friends? There was more to lose than friendship if she didn't keep her mind clear and heart safe tonight.

Glasses were again tapped and Corey made a face.

Beth felt her cheeks heat even though they laughed and cheered with the rest of the guests. She considered Nick's words to his son, admitting to the fun of kissing. Foolish girl, but Beth wanted to experience some of that fun with a certain redheaded man.

By the time dinner was over, Corey had slid down in his seat, looking bored and tired.

Beth's mom leaned toward Nick. "Would it be all right if Corey and I left? I can use Beth's car."

Nice, Mom. Real nice and obvious.

But part of her wanted to pat her mother on the back for a job well done. "Don't you want to stay for cake?"

"No." Her mom gripped her midsection. "I'm way too full. Well, Nick, what do you say?"

Nick cleared his throat. "Yeah, that's fine. Here,

take my car. It has his booster seat. I'll bring Beth home and pick up Corey."

She laid her napkin on the table and stood. "No need. I put one in Beth's car, you know, just in case." Her mom gave them a wide smile.

Beth wanted to roll her eyes.

"Might be late. Would you like me to pick up the dog?"

Nick nodded and handed over his house key. "Thank you, Mary. That'd be great. Call me if needed. You have my cell."

"Will do." She smiled. "You two have fun. Come on, Corey, let's go and get Peanut."

"Can she come to your house?"

"Sure, she can." Her mom took Corey's hand and looked back. "You two stay as late as you like."

Beth watched them leave, acutely aware of Nick sitting next to her. In the midst of a tent full of people, she felt as if they were utterly alone. "So."

He didn't bother to move over to another seat. He gave her that lopsided grin instead. "So."

She rolled her eyes.

He leaned close. "Relax. I owe you, remember?"

She hadn't forgotten. Worse, how could she exact payment without landing herself in dangerous waters?

The band had set up during dinner and the lead member announced that the bride and groom would open the floor with a first dance. Beth smiled as she watched Adam and Eva swirl in each other's arms. She'd been there when the two met, and they'd overcome so much since then.

Namely Eva's trust issues and fear.

"You look happy." Nick's voice sounded soft.

"I am. For them. Eva's a good friend."

"As you are." Nick stood and offered her his arm. "Come on."

He led her to the parquet bit of wood that served as a dance floor. A dance floor that had filled up fast. Eva's brothers were out there with their ladies, as were Eva's parents and others. Rose Marsh gave her a wave and a curious look toward Nick.

Beth waved back.

She'd introduce Nick later. For now, she wanted to pretend they had no worries. No issues. She wanted to enjoy the night on the arm of one handsome man.

The song was slow and old, but Beth recognized the tune. The lead singer purred lyrics from a Frank Sinatra hit as Nick pulled her close.

Something about flying to the moon and dancing in the stars had Beth's head spinning. She slipped her hand into Nick's, but when he tightened his hold around her waist, her breath caught.

"Relax—you're stiff as a board."

"Sorry." She settled her other hand on his shoulder, felt the solid man beneath the suit coat and concentrated on moving with Nick. "I don't dance much. Only at weddings."

He winked. "Then we've got some ground to cover."

They were at eye level, and Beth wore heels. She smiled.

Suddenly, Nick spun and then twirled her away from him only to pull her back in.

She gripped his shoulder to keep from stumbling. "Warn me next time you do that."

"Follow my lead and you'll know."

Beth furrowed her brow as it dawned on her. "Hey, wait a minute, you're good at this."

He smiled and his gray eyes crinkled at the corners.

Her stomach flipped. "Where'd you learn to dance?"

"Had to for my first undercover stint."

"Why? I don't get it."

Nick tipped his head. "Drug sales in the back of a ballroom-dancing studio."

"Oh."

A harmless answer said lightly, but it made her shiver all the same. He'd seen and done things she didn't ever want to know about. She was fooling herself if she thought they could escape what he did for a living. Not tonight. Not ever.

* * *

Nick kept Beth busy on the dance floor. The music was mixed between current and long-ago hits. They laughed with friends of hers during some of the hokier songs and finally took a break for the cutting of the cake and coffee.

Nick wolfed down his slice of marbled wedding confection in seconds flat while Beth picked at hers. Some of her hair had fallen out of its trap and hung down her soft neck past her bare shoulders. He wanted to release the rest of it.

"What?" she asked.

"Aren't you going to eat that?"

She pushed her plate toward him. "You can have it."

Nick loosened his tie. Beth fanned her face, so he pushed a glass of water toward her. "You can have my water."

"Thanks." She took a long drink. "Do you want to, um, get some fresh air?"

"Absolutely." He stood after she did, trying not to look eager to get her out of the vinyl walls of the tent.

Outside he breathed deep the chilly but sweet air from the trees in bloom surrounding them.

Beth wobbled and grabbed his arm. She slipped off her heels. "I won't get far with these things sinking in the grass."

How far did she plan on walking? "Where are we going?"

"There's a picnic table around here somewhere. I stayed with Eva for a while and I practically lived here during high school, I came over often enough. Follow me."

He did. Silently.

They reached a wooden picnic table and Beth sat on the top, her bare feet resting on the bench seat below. She rubbed her arms.

He slipped out of his jacket and handed it to her.

"Thanks." She shrugged into it.

The air was cold, but it felt good after the heated tent. Their breaths made little white puffs in front of them. He pointed to the table. "You're going to snag that dress."

"That's okay. I'll never wear it again."

"Too bad." Nick stepped closer. "You look amazing."

"Thanks." Beth snuggled deeper into his jacket, burying her hands in the pockets. "What's this?"

She'd found his string-tie restraints and pulled them out of the left side pocket.

He shrugged. "Easier to carry off duty than regular handcuffs."

"And you thought you'd apprehend someone here, at an outdoor wedding?"

He gave her a wicked grin. "Never know."

Beth's eyes widened, and then she gave him a thorough once-over. "You're carrying, aren't you?"

"I always do." Nick patted his lower back where he wore a pancake holder for his SIG Sauer. A smaller gun than his Glock, it fit well under the tuck of his shirt, where he could reach it quick, if needed.

Beth closed her eyes. "At a wedding."

"At night, in a remote place I'm not familiar with and with people I don't know. Yeah, Beth, at a wedding."

She pulled his jacket closer around her shoulders. "Did I ever tell you how my father died?"

"No." Nick looked up at the night sky filled with shimmering stars and a crescent moon.

Here it comes.

"You might have read the official report, but what really happened is that a guy he'd stopped for speeding was high on something. Instead of obeying my dad's request for his registration, the guy grabbed my father's gun and shot him." Beth talked in her usual calm teacher voice, but her eyes looked glassy.

Nick didn't know her father had been killed with his own firearm. There hadn't been a trial since the perp accepted a plea bargain and was sentenced clean as a whistle. The details of the weapon used to commit the crime had been left out. Maybe for the sake of the family or in honor of Ryken's sterling tenure, Nick didn't know.

So how did Beth know? "Who told you?"

"I overheard a couple of deputies talking at Dad's funeral. The ones who'd found him—" her voice broke "—on a dark stretch of road."

"I'm sorry, Beth." He took her cold hands in his own and chafed them softly. "Sorry for you and your dad."

"I never told my mom. She would have freaked. She'd been beside herself with worry that night when my dad didn't come home. He'd been late before, but for some reason my mom was frantic. She had called the station and I remember her screaming over the phone asking when he'd last checked in, bawling that something wasn't right. It was late when the sheriff came to our house. My father had been found dead beside his cruiser. He died alone."

"Beth—"

She sniffed and pulled her hands from his. "Don't you see why I won't go through that again?"

He brushed away a single tear with his thumb. He couldn't make her any promises, and that was what made it so tough. "I'm not your dad."

She glared at him. "You could be."

"We have something here." He pulled his jacket closed in front of her and gently tugged on the lapels, drawing her against him. "I know you feel it, too."

She surprised him by giving him a wan smile. "Why do you think I'm telling you this?"

He caressed her face. "To scare me off."

She shook her head. "No. To scare me off. To remind me why…"

"You don't date cops," he finished for her.

"Right."

"So don't call it dating." Nick searched her pretty blue eyes rimmed with dark eye shadow.

"That's not going to work."

His lips were mere seconds from hers. "We can make it work."

"We can't." But Beth's eyes drifted closed.

He touched his lips to hers and wrapped his arms around Beth's waist. *Easy, take it easy.*

Nick didn't deepen the kiss. He heard the band leader announce the bouquet toss, and the guy expressly asked for the two bridesmaids. Beth and Anne.

He couldn't keep Beth out here. "We've got to go."

Beth's eyes flew open and in them Nick saw horrified regret. Whether she regretted the interruption or kissing him, he didn't know. All he knew was that they had to get back inside that tent.

"Come on." He gave her his hand.

Beth didn't take it. She slipped on her high heels and made a sink-in-the-grass dash back where they'd come from. He followed close behind her and then took his jacket from her when they slipped through an opening in the tent.

Beth made her way onto the dance floor but hung back toward the side.

Nick noticed that Eva had been searching the group for her. The bride smiled when she spotted Beth amid the cluster of single ladies. Turning her back on them, Eva tossed the bridal bouquet behind her head. The thing had some height to it as it sailed past women literally throwing themselves forward to catch it.

But it landed.

Right in Beth's arms.

She bobbled it but managed to keep the bundle of flowers from hitting the ground. Beth looked surprised. She looked embarrassed. And then she looked at him.

Nick smiled at her. If ever he'd been given a sign about Beth being the one for him—and Corey—that was it.

Chapter Ten

"Go to dinner with me Friday night." Nick held open the passenger door for her.

"Thank you, but no." Beth plucked at a broken stem of a pink rosebud from the bridal bouquet and held it to her nose as she slid into the seat.

He started the engine and then looked at her. "Come on, Beth. Don't you think we're inevitable?"

She sighed. "Because I caught the bride's flowers and you caught the garter? Really, Nick, that's nothing but superstition."

"Maybe. Or maybe it confirms what we feel."

Beth didn't want to examine what she felt for Nick. "Look, I'm sorry if I led you on by inviting you to this wedding."

Nick smiled. "You didn't lead me on. We've been dancing around this attraction since the day we met."

He was right about that. "Doesn't mean we have to act on it."

"Too late. It's deeper now. I trust you. Especially with Corey."

Corey.... Beth closed her eyes. She'd fallen for the boy since his first day in her class.

"He needs you, Beth." Nick knew how to fight dirty without so much as raising his voice.

"That's not fair."

"Neither is your fear."

Maybe not, but it was real. The risks Nick took every day were real, too. "Have you ever considered leaving law enforcement?"

She glimpsed a flash of anger in his eyes.

"Would you leave teaching?" His voice was soft and dangerously low.

She understood where he came from. Nick's job was his calling, as teaching was hers. "No. I suppose not."

They were almost to her mom's house. The silence that settled between them in the car was louder than any radio cranked up on high volume. The space echoed with tension. And regret. At least on her part. She wanted to go out with him but knew better. What might have happened had they not been interrupted from that kiss?

Probably a good thing she didn't know.

Beth glanced at Nick driving. His lips were a grim line and his hands gripped the steering wheel.

He'd rolled up his shirtsleeves and she marveled at the steel of those lean arms. Even the hairs on his forearms were reddish-gold. She closed her eyes, remembering the feel of them wrapped around her on the dance floor.

When he kissed her...

They pulled into her mother's driveway.

"I'm sorry," Beth muttered.

Nick slammed the car in Park and turned toward her. "Yeah, me, too."

"I'll get Corey so you don't have to come in." Beth opened the door, but Nick stalled her with the touch of his hand to her shoulder. Her shoulder was encased in his jacket again.

His touch was gentle. Coaxing. "I'm not giving up."

Beth's belly flipped.

And then he gave her that lopsided grin of his. "Just so you know."

"Thanks." At least they were still friends. "I'll get your son."

The porch light came on, and Beth's mom opened the door. A sleepy-looking Corey stumbled out onto the porch. Peanut flew past him toward the car, her tail wagging furiously, but she couldn't make the jump into the backseat.

Beth bent down and picked up the little dog. Peanut cuddled right into her neck. The dog couldn't weigh more than fifteen pounds, but her belly felt bigger and more hard. "She's got to be getting close."

"Yeah. I'm afraid so."

"Hopefully, Corey will get to see the puppies born." Beth knew what an educational experience that would prove to be. She'd watched their family Lab deliver pups long ago, and she hoped Peanut waited until the end of the school day. Summer break was only two weeks away, but she didn't think the dog had that long.

Corcy climbed into his booster seat in the back, buckled in and then sprawled.

Beth settled the dog next to the drowsy boy. Her heart ached with the knowledge of what she gave up because she was too afraid to say yes to Nick.

"Good night, Beth."

"Your jacket."

"I'll get it later." He winked.

Beth shut the passenger door and watched as Nick backed out of her mother's driveway. Seconds turned into minutes, but she didn't move.

"Beth, honey. Are you coming in? It's cold out there."

It was. Beth pulled Nick's coat closer and inhaled his clean-scented aftershave, but she was already too chilled to feel any warmth from it. "Yeah. I'm coming."

She walked into her mother's house and tossed Eva's bridal bouquet on the dining room table.

"Everything all right?" Her mom's eyes shone with concern.

"Yes." Things were as they should be.

So why did she feel so horrible?

"Good night, Mom, and thanks for watching Corey." Beth kissed her mother's forehead and made her way upstairs.

Slamming her hands in the coat pockets, she felt that string restraint and frowned. It was better to feel the hurt now rather than later, after she gave everything she had to Nick only to lose him.

Wednesday morning, Beth checked her watch. Today was Occupation Day, but her first of three speakers was late. She'd asked Julie's husband, Gerry, to talk about sailing since her class had been studying historic ships of the Great Lakes.

Not to mention the biggest third-grade field trip in the fall was sailing on a tall ship out of Traverse City. Gerry must have been held up at his firm. Hopefully, the other two speakers showed.

One of them was Nick.

A knock at the door brought Thomas's father, Todd Clark, a chef by trade, peeking in the door. "Am I too early?"

Beth smiled. "Not at all. Our first speaker didn't show. Come in."

Todd brought props: his chef's hat, an apron and

what looked like the ingredients to make bread. "I'm going to need a table."

Beth stepped closer. "Can you make whatever it is you're making in twenty minutes? I have another speaker scheduled."

"It'll be tight, but yes. This is a hands-on chemistry lesson about how gluten is formed."

"Your hands on or theirs?" Beth giggled.

Todd donned his apron and hat with a smile. "Both. I brought everything I need with me, and I see you have a sink with hot and cold water. Perfect."

Beth nodded. The kids were going to love it, but not because of anything to do with chemistry. Her kids would simply want to stick their fingers in the dough.

She introduced Chef Todd and then stepped to the side to let him take over.

Leaning against the wall, she watched as Todd opened a sack of flour. He measured and then with a sinister face, Todd tossed the flour into a bowl, causing dust to fly.

Her students laughed.

Beth shook her head. Thomas's dad was quite the showman.

The kids laughed harder when Todd made more faces as he ran the water until it reached the right temperature. "Who'd like to touch this water and see how warm it feels?"

Kids swarmed.

Halfway through Chef Todd's mixing of the dough, she smelled the yeasty concoction clear across the room.

"Ewww, it smells." Gracie Cavanaugh plugged her nose.

Beth smiled. Her mom must not make home-made bread.

"That's the yeast doing its thing," Todd explained.

After some kneading, Todd separated out bits of sticky dough. "Feel it. Now add more flour—that's it. See? That's elasticity forming. The smelly yeast eating up the flour will make the dough rise."

"Oooooooh."

Beth didn't hear the door open, but she felt Nick's presence as he quietly stepped into her classroom.

"Looks like I've got a tough act to follow," he whispered.

"You've got your work cut out." She glanced at him.

Nick stood next to her, looking rigid as a soldier in his brown sheriff's uniform complete with hat.

Formidable and distant.

For a man who'd said he wasn't giving up on her, he certainly hadn't tried very hard. After the wedding, she didn't see him or Corey at church the next morning, or the rest of the day. The past two nights when Nick picked up Corey and Peanut after his shift, he hadn't stayed long.

"That's an understatement, Miss Ryken." His eyes were full of mischief and he winked at her.

Was Nick lying low on purpose? Absence makes the heart grow fonder and all that sort of thing? Clenching her jaw, Beth had to admit it had worked. She'd missed him.

Her attention was snagged by her students' clapping.

Chef Todd's demonstration was over. "Thank you, kids. Drop your dough balls into this bag. Yup, that's it."

He cleaned up his props and threw away the dough in seconds. Only the flour-covered table remained. And the yeasty smell of dough and chalky flour.

"Thank you, Mr. Clark. Don't worry about the table. I'll take care of it." She shook the man's hand and then brushed away the dusty flour left behind.

"Okay, kids, everyone wash up and then take your seats. Our next speaker is Deputy Officer Grey."

Beth heard the oohs and aahs and spotted a couple of kids poking Corey in the side. They knew Nick was his dad, but that didn't diminish the awe shining on the boy's face. Corey was proud of his father.

And Nick looked equally proud of his son, if the

softening of his features was any indication. Nick gave Corey a quick nod as he walked to the front of the room.

Once her students were seated, Beth pushed the table into the corner and then turned the time over to Nick. He started with the usual police officer speech encouraging kids to steer clear of strangers and never accept candy or a ride from anyone without their parents' approval.

He looked tall and fierce but friendly. How could he not when construction-paper sailboats hung from the ceiling over his head? His hat touched a couple as he slowly paced in front of the chalkboard, giving a brief description of his daily duties.

Looking around the room, he asked, "Any questions?"

Several hands flew in the air, so Beth picked one. "Grace."

"Do you pull over a lot of speeders?" the little girl asked.

Nick had pulled her over. She'd never forget that morning.

He glanced her way with a half smile. "Some days, yes."

The kids laughed.

Beth felt her cheeks heat. Obviously, Nick hadn't forgotten, either.

"What's the fastest speeder you ever caught?" another called out.

Nick rubbed his chin. "A man driving one hundred and twenty."

"Wow…" the students seemed to chant.

"Did he go to jail?" Grace asked.

Nick smiled. "Yes, he did."

"Did you ever shoot anyone?"

Beth cringed. A typical question, but she dreaded the answer. She glanced at Nick and waited.

Would he answer?

He looked stern. Nick's demeanor changed to very serious. "It's not like you see on TV. A police officer never brags about shooting, nor does he pull his firearm unless there's no other option. Unless he intends to use it."

The room fell silent and the kids stared at Nick with wide eyes.

"Did you ever get shot?"

"Ahh…" Nick hesitated.

Beth looked at Corey, whose face had gone pale. No way could she let Nick answer that here. Not with her heart pounding hard in her ears.

"Okay, Officer Grey, I believe our time is up. Thank you for coming." She rushed to the front of the room.

His eyes narrowed, but he nodded. "Thank you."

The kids clapped.

Beth took Nick's arm and ushered him toward the door.

"Are you trying to get rid of me?"

"For now, yes." Beth would explain later. Maybe.

Gerry stuck his head inside the room right when Beth opened the door for Nick. "Sorry I'm late."

"Oh, no, it's okay. This is Nick Grey. Nick, Gerry."

Gerry extended a hand. "You're the one sailing with us in a couple weeks. With your boy, right?"

"Yes." Nick ended the handshake.

Gerry glanced at Beth and then back at Nick with a curious smirk. "Excellent. Excellent. You'll love it. We're gone all day to the Manitou Islands. They're a beautiful place."

Nick gave her a questioning look. They hadn't gone over the details.

She'd tell him all that later, as well. She practically pushed Nick out the door. "Yeah, great. Come on, Gerry, the kids are waiting."

"Maybe Nick here wants to stay and see the slide show? See what he's in for."

Beth stopped pushing and heat flooded her face. What was wrong with her? "Do you want to stay?"

He stared at her a long time before he answered. "I'm on duty. Maybe another time."

Beth swallowed hard. "Another time."

He tipped his hat and left.

"You okay?" Gerry asked.

"Yeah. Why?"

Because she'd rudely shoved Nick out the door?

Because she was afraid of his answers to the kids' questions? Because she was falling for the guy?

Gerry shrugged. "No reason. You seem...agitated."

Beth shook her head and tried to look innocent. "No."

"You've got yourself a tall one there." Gerry patted her shoulder before making his way to the front of the class to load his DVD into the TV's player.

Beth wanted to deny it, but Nick was hers for the asking.

She glanced at Corey. The boy's color had returned and he laughed at something Thomas said. No harm done. But her stomach still roiled. Had Nick answered yes to the last question, that he'd been shot, did he know what that knowledge would do to his boy? To her?

This weekend was Memorial Day weekend—a time when folks got rowdy with the unofficial start of summer. Parties and fireworks and calls made to 911. Nick was on duty this weekend. He'd be out there on patrol. Right in the thick of it.

Nick hesitated on the porch of Mary Ryken's house. The front door was open, but a screen door stood in his way. He could hear his son's voice as he read a story about himself. Corey still hesitated and stuttered, but he could read.

Nick's heart nearly burst when he overheard Corey read the last few lines.

"I want to be a cop when I grow up, just like my dad."

"That's good, Corey. Very good." Beth's voice sounded soft. "You've earned your sailing trip, that's for sure. But you'll have to keep at it over the summer. Promise?"

Corey nodded. "I promise."

Good thing he had the following weekend off. He'd never been much of a boater and wouldn't want his son sailing the big lake without him. He rapped his knuckles on the wood of the screen door before stepping inside the warm house. "Hello?"

"Dad!" Corey tore down the hall out of the kitchen toward him.

"Hey, bud."

"Wait till you see the sailboat we're going on. It's so big and really cool!"

Nick glanced at Beth. "You could have let me stay."

Beth's pretty mouth opened but nothing came out for a second or two. "I did, but you said you were on duty."

"After you shoved me out the door." Nick gave her a playful wink. He looked around for the dog. "Where's Peanut?"

"In here on the couch in the living room sleeping." Mary looked up from knitting or whatever it was she was doing with yarn. "I think she's close to puppy time, poor thing."

"I've got the next two days off, so hopefully, they'll come then." He looked at his son. "Ready, Corey?"

"Aren't you going to eat dinner?" Corey looked confused as he glanced back and forth between them.

Did his boy notice the awkwardness between them? Probably.

Since the wedding, Nick hadn't been around much. Sunday, Susan's parents had called. They'd driven up to visit Corey and "inspect" their new house. They'd been pleased with what they'd seen, but Nick thought they might have been a little hurt from Corey's constant chatter about Miss Ryken.

Nick had explained only that she was Corey's teacher and tutor, but they saw through that. They knew Beth was someone special and not only to his boy.

The past couple of nights when he'd picked up Corey, Nick hadn't stayed. Mary had given him foil-covered plates as she used to. All because Nick could barely stand being in the same room with Beth and not pulling her close.

He was falling pretty hard.

"I don't know, bud." He looked at Beth. Did she want him to stay?

She'd been in a hurry for him to leave her class

this morning. She'd been rattled pretty good by her students' questions, too. He could tell. What would she do if she saw the old bullet wound on his shoulder or the knife stab in his lower back?

"Mom made spaghetti," she said. "And it's best served straight from the pot."

He thought spaghetti tasted better reheated, but then, his had always come from a store-bought jar. "I'll stay."

"Corey, how about a game of Battleship?" Mary peered over her glasses at him. "You two go ahead. We've eaten."

His son jumped at the chance to play his favorite game, and Nick knew a setup when he saw it. He didn't mind. He gave Mary a grateful nod and followed Beth into the kitchen.

Silently, he washed his hands at the sink while Beth served up plates and set them on the table.

"What do you want to drink? Milk, water or pop?"

He sat down and sprinkled cheese atop his pasta and sauce, which smelled better than anything he'd ever made. "Water's fine."

Beth brought two iced glasses of water and sat down.

He took her hand and bowed his head. "Thank You, Lord, for this food, and show us that there's nothing to fear in You. Amen."

Beth slipped her hand from his. "Nice."

He didn't miss her sarcasm. "You fear what I do, but I'm in God's hands every day. You are, too. And Corey. Your mom."

"What about my dad?"

"He was, too." Nick took a bite of spaghetti and closed his eyes. "This is good."

Beth nodded. "My mom's got skills."

He chuckled. Beth did, too. She'd taught his son to read, to laugh again and show his love. For that Nick would always be grateful.

He sighed. "I don't have the answer why your dad was killed. I don't know why Susan had the troubles she did or why it all ended wrapped around a tree one night. All I know is that we're not meant to live in fear."

Beth nodded and they ate in silence.

"You've been shot before, haven't you?" Beth whispered.

He nodded around another mouthful. "Yeah."

Beth closed her eyes tight.

He kept his voice low so Corey wouldn't hear. "It was a random bullet during a domestic dispute. I got in the way."

"And that's supposed to make it okay?" Beth's eyes went wide. "Does Corey know?"

Nick shook his head. "When he's older, I'll tell him like my dad told me."

Beth looked at him. "Is your dad alive?"

"No—"

She pushed her plate aside and gripped her forehead. "And now you've got another Grey who wants to join the force."

"My father died from cancer."

"Oh."

He reclaimed her hand. "Beth, life's fleeting. We're not supposed to get too comfy down here, right? We've got to make our days count for as many as God gives us. Count yours with me." He caressed the back of her hand with his thumb. "And Corey."

She didn't look convinced, but Nick had made a dent in her resolve. There was no need to rush things. He'd pleaded his case. He'd give Beth some space for it to sink in.

He wiped his mouth with a napkin. "Now, tell me about this sailing trip."

"Well, it's fun, and the boat is really nice with a cabin and galley. Gerry's a good sailor. He's been sailing all his life."

"We'll be gone all day?"

Beth nodded. "You'll need swimwear, sunscreen and something warm to slip on in case it gets cool."

Nick nodded. "Where are we going again?"

"South Manitou Island. You'll love it."

He'd love spending the day with Beth on a beach. But sailing? He'd never been a big fan. Seemed like too much work.

"After school's out?" He'd know by then if Corey

had legitimately passed second-grade reading. He didn't want to force advancement to the third, but he would if he had to. Corey needed to move forward, not step back.

"The weekend right before."

"Something to look forward to, then."

Chapter Eleven

Beth couldn't sit still while Corey read. She paced her classroom, listening and not listening. Her mind wandered to thoughts of Nick.

They were all in God's hands.

She knew that on an intellectual level, but deep down did she really? Did she trust God with what she couldn't control—her future? She sighed.

"Something wrong, Miss Ryken? Did I miss a word?" the boy asked.

She looked into gray eyes that were so like his father's. "Oh, no. You're doing very well. I think we can call it a day."

Her cell phone rang and she grabbed it on the third ring. It was Nick. "Hello?"

"Hey, can you bring Corey home? Peanut's water broke, so I don't want to leave her alone." Nick sounded nervous.

Beth smiled. "We're on our way. Need anything?"

"Just you, here. I don't know what I'm doing."

Beth let loose a soft laugh even as his words gave her butterflies. "Don't worry, Peanut knows what to do. See you in a few."

At the mention of the dog's name, Corey stopped shoving books into his backpack. "What's wrong with Peanut?"

"It's puppy time. Let's go."

Corey grinned and scrambled for the door.

Beth hurried right behind him.

She tapped her mom's name in her phone and then cradled it against her ear. "Hey. Peanut's water broke, so I'm taking Corey home. I don't know how long I'll be."

Her mom laughed. "Take your time, honey. This is so exciting. Let me know what she has, okay?"

"Will do." Beth disconnected. Stuffing the phone back in her purse, she opened the car door for Corey.

He threw his backpack inside before climbing into his backseat booster chair.

"Buckled?" Beth checked before slipping in behind the wheel.

"Yup."

She pulled out of the parking lot and headed for Nick's. It didn't take long. Once there, Beth and Corey raced through the side door that led from the laundry room to the kitchen.

"Nick?" Beth called out to let him know they were there.

He sat at the kitchen table with messy hair. His feet were bare beneath loose cotton pants and a T-shirt. He looked up, relieved. "She keeps pacing."

Beth watched Peanut. Sure enough, the little dog panted and paced. She scratched at the bedding on the floor in the kitchen and lay down only to get back up again.

Corey sat on the linoleum floor and the dog crawled into his lap and settled down. But only for a few moments. She got back up and paced some more.

Beth looked at the huge pile of bedding. Afternoon sunshine streamed in through the sliding glass door onto the blankets. Peanut loved to lie in the sun, but maybe not today. Not now. "We should set her bed in a quieter place. What about your room?"

Nick scrunched his face. "I've got carpet."

"Do you have a kiddie pool?"

Corey bounced up. "It's in the garage."

"We'll make up a bed for her in the pool in your room and close the blinds. I think she needs quiet."

They got busy getting the pool down from the garage rafters, cleaned it thoroughly and then set everything up in Nick's room.

Beth drew the blinds while Nick carried Peanut in followed by Corey.

Beth checked her watch. It was getting close to dinnertime. "Maybe if we leave her alone for a bit, things will start moving."

"And we'll have puppies?" Corey asked.

Nick tousled his boy's hair. "That's the plan."

"Got plans for dinner? I can make something quick," Beth offered. Corey had to be hungry.

"How's frozen pizza sound?"

Beth glanced at Corey, who was inching down the hallway to peek into Nick's room. "Sounds perfect. I'll make a salad, too, if you have the stuff."

"I do." Nick spotted Corey, too. "Come on, bud. Give Peanut some space."

Half an hour later, Beth finished slicing veggies for a salad while the pizza baked in the oven. Corey was in Nick's room checking on Peanut, but there was still no hint of puppies. Nick was scanning the internet for information on dog deliveries when the oven timer sounded.

Beth turned off the oven and set the bowl of salad on the table. "Find anything?"

Nick's face looked grim. "Lots of stuff."

Beth walked over to stand behind him. "Like what?"

"Puppies are supposed to be born within minutes of a dog's water breaking."

Beth leaned over Nick's shoulder to read the website page, and dread filled her. "How long has it been?"

"Too long." Nick pointed to the screen. "Says here that after two hours call the vet."

Beth chewed her bottom lip. It had been at least that long since Nick had called her at school. "Corey should eat something. I'll have him wash up while you call your vet."

Nick nodded.

Beth headed down the hall and peered through the door to Nick's room. Corey lay on the floor and stroked the little dog's head. Peanut appeared calm. No more panting or pacing. No sign of puppies coming, either.

She could hear Nick's muffled voice as he talked on the phone. "Corey, it's time for dinner. You need to wash up."

"Okay." The boy dashed for the bathroom.

Beth knelt beside the kiddie pool in the corner of Nick's darkened room. A heavy-laden Peanut looked so small amid a swirl of blankets in that big blue plastic circle.

"How is she?" Nick knelt next to her and scratched beneath the dog's chin.

"Calm as can be. What did the vet say?"

Nick's eyes looked worried. "He'll meet us at his office in half an hour."

"Did he say anything else?"

"Only that time's not on our side."

Beth closed her eyes. That didn't sound good. Not good at all.

* * *

Nick glanced at Corey through the rearview mirror. His boy sat in the backseat with Beth. Peanut lay on a couple towels in Beth's lap and nudged under her hand for more pats. The dog acted as if nothing was wrong. He knew better. He'd read the online articles.

"Is Peanut going to die?" Corey's eyes were grave.

Nick wanted to lie, say everything would be fine and erase that crease of worry in his son's forehead. "I don't know, son. Let's pray that she doesn't."

Corey nodded. "We prayed for Mom."

"I know." Nick's stomach turned.

He glanced at Beth through the mirror. Her eyes watered as she looked back.

Nick and his son had prayed in the emergency waiting room the day of Susan's accident. Along with her parents, they'd all prayed. Susan had still died. How did he explain why to a seven-year-old?

"Take my hand, Corey." Beth's voice sounded thin. "Dear Lord, please touch our little Peanut and her pups. Bring her through this. Amen."

"Amen," Corey echoed.

Nick kept praying, though, begging God not to take his boy's dog. Wasn't losing his mother enough?

He glanced again at Beth. She felt like an anchor here. Calm in the face of the storm ahead. Her eyes were closed and she held Corey's hand. Both petted the dog, but Beth continued to pray. Silently. He could see her lips move.

They pulled into the veterinarian's office and Nick shut off the engine. Corey was already out of his booster chair and tearing around the other side of the car reaching for Peanut.

"I've got her, bud." Nick lifted the little dog from Beth and held her close. Peanut nuzzled under his chin and Nick patted the dog's back.

His eyes burned. It had to be okay.

Beth got out and Corey reached for her hand. She took it and the two walked into the vet's ahead of him.

Please, God. Let Peanut live.

"It's going to be okay, Corey." Beth wrapped her arms around a very worried little boy.

He melted into her embrace.

They sat on the same vinyl-covered bench in the lobby where they'd been given the bad news. Corey had heard it right along with her and Nick, and the boy's eyes had gone wide as marbles. A no-nonsense kind of man in his sixties, the country vet didn't mince words. Peanut's contractions had stopped, and while she was not distressed, her puppies' heartbeats were tragically low. Much lower than what he liked for a C-section. Lower than those of puppies expected to live.

After hearing their options, Nick wanted to try the shots that should induce labor. So they waited. And waited.

The office loomed silent. Even the dogs in the back that had been barking quieted down. An exotic bird in a cage behind the desk nodded off, too. No more swaying from foot to foot. Could animals tell when one of their own was in trouble? The silence lingered, interrupted only by the tick-tick of the giant clock over the doorway.

Beth let her head fall back against the wall. Corey had curled up on the bench and his head rested in her lap. She ran her fingers through the kid's hair. So much for staying in teacher mode. Beth had moved right into comforter.

Like a mom.

"I'll be right back." Nick stood and exited the office.

"Where's he going?" Corey asked.

"I don't know." Beth watched Nick on his phone as he paced outside in front of the plate-glass window. Who was he calling?

After a few minutes, Nick stepped back inside. He crouched down in front of Corey. "I called the pastor, bud. We've got the church praying for Peanut."

Corey lifted his head and gave his dad a brave smile.

And Beth's heart broke.

A gut-wrenching sound suddenly came from the back, making the hairs on her arms rise.

The dogs started barking again and the bird fluttered against its cage and squawked.

Beth looked at Nick. "Was that Peanut?"

"It must be."

Corey sat up with wide eyes and a white face.

She didn't remember her Lab screaming when she delivered her puppies. What if these puppies were too big to come out?

Beth pulled Corey close. Whether to soothe the boy's fear or her own, she wasn't sure. "It's okay, Corey. Keep praying. God's with us. He's always with us."

"How do you know?" His seven-year-old voice was raw.

She brushed back his bangs. "Because the Bible tells us so. And so does your dad."

"She's right, bud." Nick wrapped his arms around them both and hung on.

This was what families did. They clung to each other in times of trouble. Beth closed her eyes and kept praying.

Fifteen minutes later, the vet came out with a big smile on his face. "Mr. Grey, we've got our first puppy and it's alive. Shocked my socks off. Born back feet first. I had to help pull the pup out. Little thing was clogging up the whole process. Come on back. I think you're in for a treat."

Corey jumped up.

He and Nick followed the vet. But then Nick turned. "Are you coming?"

Beth shook her head. Peanut was their dog. This was a moment Nick should have with his son. She needed the distance. "You two go ahead."

Nick stared a moment longer.

Corey peeked around the corner and pulled on Nick's hand. "Come on, Dad."

Beth smiled. "Go ahead. I have an e-reader in my purse and I need to call my mom. I'll be fine."

Nick disappeared with his boy and all was quiet again, save for the murmurs of him and Corey and the vet in the next room and the occasional yip from the dogs boarded in back. No more screaming from Peanut.

Beth slumped in her seat, her stomach a mess of knots that wouldn't loosen. "Thank You, Lord."

Another half hour passed and the vet came out to get her. "They'd like you to come back. Peanut's doing great."

Beth took a deep breath and let it out with a whoosh. Grabbing her purse, she followed the vet into the dimly lit examining room. Peanut lay on several towels on the floor with three squirming little puppies around her. A heat lamp had been turned on overhead, warming the entire area.

Nick sat on the floor a short distance away and Corey lay on his belly next to him.

When she entered, Nick looked up at her with shining eyes. "We're waiting for one more."

Beth glanced at the vet, feeling sorry for pulling the old man away from his evening. The animal doctor didn't seem to mind. He gave her a cheerful nod and left the room whistling. No doubt to attend to his office business or the dogs in back while they watched the wonder of puppy birth.

Nick held out his hand. "Come here."

She set her purse on the floor. Without taking his hand, Beth sat on the floor beside Corey.

Corey sat up. "Isn't this cool? Four puppies."

Where had that little dog stowed four pups all these weeks? "Wow."

Nick grinned. "Yeah, right. Wow."

Beth smiled.

Peanut didn't notice them much. She was busy sniffing and licking her three puppies, nuzzling them as they wiggled and latched on to nurse.

Beth glanced at Nick over Corey's head. God had given them a huge blessing. No, five blessings if they included the arrival of Peanut. That little dog had helped bond father and son. Watching Corey lean against his father's arm, Beth's eyes stung. They'd healed. They were going to be okay.

Peanut got up, turned a couple of times and then moved away from her pups. The puppies wobbled and rolled around and the last little blessing made its appearance. Another puppy slipped out in a matter of seconds, black-and-white nose first. And Peanut got to work cleaning up the last baby.

Nick chuckled. "That's it, then. They're all accounted for."

"Amen." It was all Beth could manage around the lump of emotion in her throat. God had saved Corey's dog and she was grateful.

He hadn't saved Nick's wife, though. What had Nick gone through with his son as they'd waited in a different kind of hospital not so long ago? They'd made it through. Battle scarred for sure, but they'd made it.

Could she?

By the time they pulled out of the vet's and headed for home, Peanut had been x-rayed to make sure nothing had been left behind. The puppies were checked over and sexed. Peanut had three girls and one boy—all were given a clean bill of health.

Nick would receive his bill in the mail, but the guy didn't even blink at the cost. It was much less than it could have been. Much better outcome, too.

Corey sat in the back with a box holding Peanut and her puppies next to him. "What are we going to name them?"

"Whatever you want." Nick smiled at his son through the rearview mirror.

"I don't know any girl names."

"We could name them different kinds of nuts like their mom."

Corey laughed. "What other kinds of nuts?"

"Almond or Hazelnut or Cashew or even Filbert."

Corey laughed harder. "Or Walnut."

Nick laughed. "Sure, why not?"

Beth stared out the window into the darkness that settled over cherry orchards that had lost their white blooms. Nick grabbed her hand with a squeeze. She looked at him.

"What do you think?"

Beth tried to sound cheerful. "What about Brittle, Butter, Cookie and Cake?"

Nick gave her an odd look. "I think we'll come up with something." He threaded his fingers through hers. "Thank you."

She squeezed back before pulling away. He needed both hands on the wheel for the upcoming curve in the road. "You're welcome."

"I mean it, Beth. You've done a lot for us. This weekend I'm taking Corey to stay with his grandparents while I'm on duty. Would you go with me? You know, so you can meet them."

"Let me think about it." Beth had to admit she was curious about them, but meeting them was a big step. Maybe in the wrong direction.

She peeked in the backseat. Corey's head bobbed against his chest as sleep took him. "He's done in."

"Corey was a trouper through all this because you were his anchor tonight. He needed you. I needed you, too."

"Thanks." What else could she say? The whole way home, Beth couldn't stop envisioning a different kind of scene—one with Nick in the hospital instead. How would Corey deal with that after losing his mom?

They pulled into Nick's garage. Beth sat in her seat a moment while Nick unbuckled and then lifted Corey out of his seat. She got out and grabbed the box of dog and puppies while Nick carried his son.

They entered through the laundry room without a word. He walked down the hall to settle Corey into bed, and Beth transferred Peanut and her pups into the blanketed kiddie pool.

The dog licked her hand and then turned her back, shielding her puppies from view.

"Okay, Mama, I'll give you some space." Beth understood those feelings. "You're a good girl, Peanut. A good mama, too."

Beth left the door open and headed for the kitchen. She'd managed to put the salad and pizza in the fridge before they'd left, but the sink was a mess with all her veggie clippings. She scooped up the waste into a plastic grocery bag and threw it in the garbage.

She washed her hands and then rinsed a clean

cloth to wipe down the counter. Corey's face kept coming back to her. A scared, wide-eyed little boy who'd waited so bravely for news of his dog. Was he brave because he'd been through this before with his mom?

Why did some live and others die?

Beth's vision blurred. She leaned against the counter and closed her eyes against the burning tears, but they leaked out anyway.

"Hey, hey…." Nick was behind her.

She hadn't heard him come into the kitchen.

He rubbed her shoulders with strong hands that moved softly. "Beth, honey, what's going on?"

Beth shook her head, her throat so tight she coughed.

He turned her around and pulled her into his arms.

She welcomed his embrace. Took the warmth he gave, but that was all she'd take. Who was she trying to fool? She fought a losing battle if she thought she could keep herself from falling for him.

"It's okay. Everything's okay now."

But it wasn't.

He pulled back and looked into her face and rubbed away tears on her cheeks with his thumbs. "Why are you crying?"

She shook her head and sniffed.

Would he be angry if she told him? He'd made it clear he wouldn't leave law enforcement. Whining about it now was no better than nagging. Beth didn't want to do either.

She hunted behind her for the roll of paper towels they'd used for napkins at dinner. She grabbed one and wiped her face, blew her nose.

Nick chuckled, but he hadn't let go of her. His arms hung loosely around her waist. He gave her a gentle shake. "Tell me."

"I, ah, I don't know what I would have done if we'd lost Peanut." Beth couldn't come clean.

She couldn't share the visions she'd had of a worried Corey in a hospital waiting room. Didn't Nick realize the impact on his son if he were injured—or worse—from his job? Sure, he'd moved to where he thought it was safe, but Beth's father had thought the same thing. She and her mom had, too.

He narrowed his gaze. "We didn't."

She looked away.

Nick cupped her cheeks and searched her eyes. "What's going on in that beautiful head of yours?"

"I don't deal with loss very well," she managed.

"We didn't lose the dog, or her pups."

"But we could have." Her voice broke.

He ran a hand through her hair. "You're stronger than you realize, Beth."

She felt ready to crack into pieces. "I don't know about that...."

"I do."

"What if—"

He traced her bottom lip with his fingertip. "Stop thinking about all the what-ifs. You won't lose me."

She clung to that promise.

Nick tipped up her chin and kissed her. Really kissed her.

And she kissed him back.

The tidal wave of feelings hit hard, weakening her resolve to pull back when he deepened their kiss.

She loved Nick.

She loved Corey, too, and more than anything she wanted to protect that boy from any more losses. But how, when she couldn't even protect herself?

Chapter Twelve

"You got home late last night." Beth's mom scrambled eggs with a whisk and then poured the mixture into a hot skillet. "Want some breakfast?"

"Sure." Beth sat down, rubbing her eyes.

"Everything okay?"

Beth nodded a little too quickly.

Her mom turned off the burner, brought two cups of coffee to the table and sat down across from her. She couldn't fool her mom, who narrowed her gaze with concern. "Tell me, honey. What's wrong?"

Nick had called her honey. And later, when she'd left his house, he'd told her that she'd brought sweetness to his and his son's life.

Beth closed her eyes a couple of seconds before zeroing in on her mother. "If you had the chance to go back, knowing what would happen to Dad, would you have married him anyway?"

Her mother smiled. "You're in love with Nick."

Beth took a sip from her steaming mug. "It takes more than love to make it work. You've said so yourself."

"True." She patted her hand. "Hmm, what's this all about, Beth?"

Beth continued to sip the gourmet coffee from the coffee club her mother had signed up for. She received regular shipments every month. Too expensive by far, but Beth had to admit it sure tasted good.

They'd never talked about how her father's death had impacted her mom. It had always been the elephant in the room. Sure, Beth got on her mom about her spending habits and frivolous purchases, but she'd never examined too closely the core reason for them. Beth had been afraid to ask her mom to seek help. She'd been afraid to point out the obvious, as well. Her mom used shopping to fill the void left in the wake of her husband's death.

Her mother's eyes filled with tears. "The pain of losing a spouse well before their time is something I wouldn't wish on anyone."

It hurt to hear her mother's voice so thick with emotion. "It's okay, Mom. You don't have to talk about it."

Her mother grabbed her hand and gently squeezed. "You need to hear it, Beth. I know you miss your dad. I do, too. And it still stings, even after all this time. I think about him every day."

Her mom took a sip of her own coffee. "Sometimes I find myself looking forward to telling your father something when he gets home. Like when Peanut followed Corey. Your father would have loved that little dog."

Beth's eyes blurred.

"But I'll see him again. You will, too, Beth. Death is never final."

She nodded and a tear leaked out.

Her mom patted her hand. "To answer your question, yes, I would gladly marry your father a hundred times over, even though I've never felt equipped to handle his death. I'd do it all over again."

Beth wondered if maybe her mother was far better equipped than she'd ever thought. It was Beth who was the coward here.

"If you want to build a future with Nick and Corey, you need to prepare for the worst but hope for the best. And God is our hope."

Her mom's words echoed something Nick had said before. That was the way he prepared for his workday. He prepared for the worst. He truly believed he was in God's hands.

We're all in God's hands.

Even so, Nick carried a gun off duty. Proof of his readiness to act in any given situation. Being a cop was part of who he was, not simply what he did for a living. She'd have to accept that. Embrace it, even.

"Has Nick told you how he feels?"

Beth shrugged. Her heart whirled at the memory of his kisses and the way he'd made her feel. Protected and cherished.

Loved.

Her mom chuckled softly. "Well, it's obvious he's crazy about you. Corey is, too."

Beth ran her fingertip around the rim of her mug. "Tonight Nick's taking Corey to his grandparents' for the long weekend since he'll be working extended shifts. He wants me to go with him."

"Will you?"

"I would like to meet them." Beth didn't add that she wanted to see for herself if they were worthy of caring for Corey in case something happened to Nick.

In case Beth couldn't follow through on her feelings.

Her mother looked at her long and hard. "Beth, this isn't something you can figure out with your head. You have to pray for God's leading and then follow your heart. That's where He'll speak to you. Inside your heart, you'll know, but you have to trust that small voice. Listen for it and you'll hear."

"I'll try." That was all she could commit to.

For now.

* * *

That afternoon, Nick stepped into Mary Ryken's dining room. The familiar scent of cinnamon and melted butter hung in the air as always. "Ready, bud?"

His son shifted his backpack on his narrow shoulders. "What about Peanut and the puppies?"

"They'll be fine at home. I'll check on them during my rounds." He glanced at Mary, who held a plastic container of cookies to take with them on the two-hour trip south to Susan's parents'.

"Beth will be right down," Mary said. "And Corey had a PB&J and milk and cookies after school."

"Thanks."

His son ate better afternoon snacks than Nick typically ingested for lunch. Today was no exception. The hot dog he'd wolfed down lay like a lead pipe in his gut.

He waited for Beth. Was she going with them? She'd never said for sure the night before. But then, he'd never given her the chance to answer before kissing her good-night.

Nick rubbed the back of his neck.

He wanted Susan's parents to know that he'd not only moved on, but he was settling down for real. They'd seen his house, and he wanted them to meet the woman who would be a good mom to his boy, their grandson.

If Beth agreed to take up the role.

As usual, Nick put the cart before the horse, thinking about a lifetime ahead when they hadn't gone out yet. He may have kissed Beth only last night, but he already had them married. Would she have him?

"Hi."

He looked up to see her coming down the stairs dressed in long denim shorts and a pretty yellow top. A light blue sweater hung over her arm. Her purse dangled from the other.

And his heart took a nosedive.

Beth had better have him, because he wanted her. No matter how long it took, Nick made a silent vow he'd convince her to give them a chance. Somehow.

"Hi." His fingers itched to touch her.

"Thanks for inviting me along." Beth was at the bottom step.

"Thanks for going." Nick couldn't help it. He tucked a strand of her blond hair behind her ear and let his fingers swipe her jaw.

Beth's cheeks went pink and she looked away. And turned toward Corey. "Are you looking forward to visiting your grandparents?"

"I guess." His boy shrugged.

Nick tried to shake off the awkwardness that had bloomed overnight between them. "Well, let's go, then."

Mary gave him a knowing smile and that gave him hope. As the wife of a cop killed on duty, Mary must have good advice for her daughter. The right advice. But then, Mary hadn't been excited about him being a deputy, either. He didn't need any more strikes against him.

"Not sure when I'll have her back." Nick made it sound like a date. Maybe it would be. If they stopped somewhere for dinner on the way home.

"No worries." Mary's smile was broader yet.

He hoped so.

Beth gave her mom a sharp look.

Mary trusted him, but he wasn't sure about Beth. Her fear kept her rolled up tight as a ball of string, and Nick couldn't find the end in order to unravel it. Beth needed a little unraveling.

By the time they made it to his former in-laws' house, they'd discussed at length possible names for the puppies. Corey wanted to name them after colors—Blue, Pink, Periwinkle and Red. Nick still pulled for nut names, and Beth thought the puppies should be called Disney character names. Having nothing agreed, they played a rousing game of word rhymes that had eaten up the travel time.

Beth never stopped being a teacher. But then, he never stopped being a cop.

"This is lovely," Beth whispered as they pulled into the driveway.

"Yeah." Nick stared at the small farmhouse

situated on a large lot in a small village north of Grand Rapids. He'd never given it much notice before. Every other time he'd come here, he'd been in some sort of turmoil—job or Susan related. Now he noticed the flowers that grew in clumps along the walkway. Mary would like them.

"There's a bunch of cider mills and apple orchards around here." He and Susan had gotten in an argument at one. Ruined the day, too.

"Similar to home." Beth smiled, but she looked tense.

"Yeah, sort of." Nick stalled her with a touch of his hand to her elbow. "Relax—they won't bite."

Susan's parents were standing at the front door. "Corey!"

"Hi, Grandma." His boy ran into his grandmother's arms.

"You sure about that?" Beth whispered.

"I got your back." Nick walked forward and extended his hand to his former father-in-law. "Greg, this is Beth Ryken. Corey's teacher and tutor."

"Nice to meet you." His father-in-law shook Beth's hand and shared a look with his wife. "Ellen, this is Beth."

"Hello."

Beth offered her hand to Ellen, who accepted it politely, but the two women sized each other up. Beth towered over his short and stout mother-in-law, but the women didn't seem to notice differences in stature. Like a couple of cats squaring off, the two stared hard at each other.

Ellen broke eye contact first. "Come in, please."

Corey had already raced into the house straight for the exotic saltwater aquarium.

As they followed his former in-laws inside, Nick hoped this didn't turn out to be a bad idea, forcing Susan's parents to meet the new woman in his life. Forcing anything never worked. He should know that by now.

Once inside, Ellen turned to Beth. "Would you like the tour? Corey's got his own room here—for when he visits."

"I'd like that." Beth followed his mother-in-law up the stairs, but she glanced at him.

Nick gave her a nod of encouragement as he watched them go up the rest of the way. Following Greg into the kitchen, he asked, "Are they going to be okay up there?"

Greg chuckled. "Ellen looked forward to meeting Corey's tutor. She won't knock her out. Yet. Are you serious about this woman?"

His father-in-law didn't mince words. Neither did Nick. "I am."

"Hmm. And Corey likes her?"

Nick narrowed his gaze. "He does."

"Kind of soon, don't you think?"

"It's been over a year now." Nick had mourned enough.

Greg shook his head. "Not what I meant. You've known this woman how long?"

"Two months."

Greg nodded but kept quiet.

Twice as long as he'd known Susan before they ran off and eloped. But he got the point. Loud and clear.

Corey joined them in the kitchen. "Hey, Dad, can I watch TV?"

Nick looked at his son. "Ask your grandfather."

"For a few minutes. I need your help in the garden before dinner." Greg looked at Nick. "Are you staying?"

Nick shook his head. "I was hoping to take Beth to dinner on our way back."

He looked forward to alone time with her. Find out where he stood, where they were headed.

Susan's parents were by no means old, only in their early sixties, but they were wise. Maybe Greg was right and it was too soon. Maybe Nick needed to relax and let the relationship develop on its own.

His former in-laws had Susan and then her brother later in life. Ellen had retired early in order to care for Corey after Susan's death. She was a finicky woman, and that intrusion into their ordered and unhurried life had no doubt taken some getting used to. But Nick never doubted how much Susan's parents loved Corey.

Greg opened the fridge. "How 'bout some iced tea while we wait for the women?"

"Sure." Nick scratched his temple and looked up at the ceiling, hearing the creaks in the floor of the women walking around up there. How long was this tour going to take?

Beth followed Ellen into each room while she explained that they'd moved here after Susan married Nick and their son had joined the military. A quiet place to retire, Ellen had said. Beth was glad that Nick's late wife hadn't grown up here. Fewer painful memories for everyone. But Susan's memory lingered like cloying perfume. Pictures were everywhere.

"This is Corey's room."

Beth stepped into the boyishly decorated bedroom with its race-car bed and NASCAR curtains. Corey wasn't into NASCAR. He liked baseball and sailboats and puppies. "Did Nick tell you their dog had puppies?"

Ellen smiled with surprise. "He didn't. How many?"

"Three girls and one boy. They haven't named them yet. Can't agree on what to call them."

Ellen chuckled. "Corey loves animals, but I won't deal with the mess. That's why we have fish. They're Greg's hobby."

Expensive hobby. Ellen's home might be spotless, but Beth would rather have dog hair and PB&J fingerprints on the fridge. As an elementary teacher, Beth was used to her noisy, messy world. Bright and vibrant.

Her gaze caught on a picture resting atop a dresser. Like a marionette on a string, Beth stepped closer as if pulled. The family portrait was recent. Corey looked only a little younger, but Nick's hair was long and wavy.

He'd worked undercover then and he looked like a dude with a 'tude in that picture. Nick's arm was draped around a very thin blonde wearing a lot of makeup and poufed-up hair. Fussy. Susan looked high maintenance.

"That's my daughter, Susan. You sort of resemble her."

Beth backed up. That was a weird thing to say. She glanced at Ellen, looking for clues that weren't there. "You think so?"

Ellen cocked her head. "No, maybe not."

Beth studied the portrait harder, but only for seconds. They had the same coloring perhaps, but Beth wasn't anywhere near as coiffed. Her features were not as perfectly chiseled, either.

She glanced at Ellen. "I'm sorry for your loss."

"Thank you. It hasn't been easy. Especially letting Corey go."

Beth swallowed hard. What did she mean? "I'm sure. He's a wonderful boy."

"Nick told us how well you've tutored him. Greg and I appreciate all that you've done. Corey showed us his storybooks when we visited and mentioned a sailing trip?"

Beth nodded. "Friends of mine sail, and Corey earned the chance to go. Nick agreed that it'd be good for him to work toward a reward instead of against the threat of repeating second grade."

"Will he?"

Beth cocked her head. "What?"

"Pass second grade."

Beth had to remember to stay in teacher mode, but it was tough. She was the grandmother, and Beth wasn't sure how much Nick had shared with the woman.

But under this grandmother's scrutiny, Beth believed blunt honesty was best. "He's borderline considering his reading level. Nick wouldn't agree to hold him back."

Ellen's direct gaze pierced her. "What do you think?"

"I think Corey's not done. He needs to work hard this summer to prepare for third grade and the testing he'll face. What made you pull him out of school?"

Ellen's expression clouded over. "I wasn't very good at homeschooling, but I couldn't leave him in that school where he'd been so lost and alone. He cried every day."

Beth's heart twisted, remembering what Diane had said. Poor kid. He missed his mother and wanted a new one. He wanted a whole family. He'd been so withdrawn when he first came, but with Thomas and Gracie and her mother he'd blossomed. Why hadn't they looked for a different school? One that could better meet Corey's needs? But then, they were grieving, too. Maybe having Corey home was a way to hold on to their daughter's memory a little longer.

"He needed us," Ellen added. "He still needs us."

Beth nodded, feeling a little lost herself. "Of course. You were there for him when he needed you most."

Ellen gave her a curt nod.

Stupid thing to say to a grandparent. Of course they'd been there. They'd always be there, too. Especially if Nick wasn't. Ellen made that perfectly clear.

Beth glanced back at the picture. She thought about Susan breaking those plates and Corey's reaction when Beth had roughly set her mom's table. They did look a little bit alike in a relative sort of way. Weird. Was that why Corey had been at ease with her that first day in school?

Ellen's smile was tight. "I loved my daughter, but I'd be lying if I didn't admit that she put Nick through a lot. Put us all through a lot."

"I'm so sorry."

"I wouldn't have blamed Nick had he left Susan, but he didn't. Not with Corey so young." Ellen gave her a pointed look. "Nick came from a broken home."

Beth hadn't known that. There was a lot about Nick she didn't know, but she knew what kind of man he was. A man with a mother-in-law who defended him. "He's a good father."

Ellen nodded. "Corey needs him now more than ever. My grandson needs stability in his life."

Beth agreed.

Ellen wasn't only stating the obvious here. She sent a message. One Beth didn't have much trouble deciphering. Ellen might not welcome another woman stepping in to raise her grandson, but she wouldn't stand for her grandson or Nick being jerked around. Or hurt.

"We're here if anything happens to threaten that stability."

"Of course." Beth swallowed.

Would Susan's parents fight for Corey if something ever happened to Nick? They were the boy's flesh and blood. They seemed like good people, solid and respectable. But anything was possible when it came to a question of custody.

Beth followed Ellen back downstairs, where Nick waited for her on the deck with an empty glass in his hand. Exiting through the sliding glass door, she spotted Corey helping his grandfather in the garden. They stuck fat wooden markers into the soil, labeling the seeds and seedlings planted in neat rows.

Would Corey be lonely growing up here? He'd made friends at school and had a dog with puppies. Would Ellen take Peanut along with the boy?

The knot in Beth's stomach pulled tighter.

"We better get going." Nick called out to Corey. "We're leaving, bud."

The boy waved, unfazed. "See you later."

Nick smiled.

"Corey, you should give your father a hug." Ellen stood next to Nick.

"It's okay."

Beth bit her lip. She agreed with Ellen but didn't say a word. It wasn't her place.

Corey trotted up onto the deck and Nick gave his son a bear hug, squeezing tight until Corey squirmed and squealed with laughter. "Bye, Dad."

"See you in a couple days."

Corey nodded and then launched himself at her. "Bye, Miss Ryken."

Beth hesitated before returning the little boy's embrace. She hugged him tight and fought the urge to kiss his forehead. "Bye, Corey. Have fun, okay?"

"Yup." He broke away and ran to join his grandfather back in the garden.

She glanced at Ellen. The woman's gaze was cool, but Beth reached out her hand. "Nice to meet you."

Ellen took it for a brief shake, her smile polite. "You, too."

She felt Nick's hand at the small of her back.

"Let's go. Thanks, Ellen. I'll call you when I leave to pick up Corey."

"Perfect, we'll meet you halfway."

"Sounds good."

Beth didn't think Ellen was a meet-halfway kind of woman. She got her way or worked hard until she did. Maybe Susan had rebelled against that. Had she married Nick to spite her staid parents?

Beth couldn't wait to get out of there.

Nick glanced at Beth in the passenger seat. She sat quietly straight with her hands in her lap. A quiet Beth was a troubled one.

"Okay, spill it."

She looked at him with wide eyes. "Spill what?"

"What's on your mind. You haven't said a word since we left."

"Do I remind you of your first wife?"

Where had that question come from?

"No, not really. There's a slight similarity with

your blond hair and blue eyes, but that's where it ends. You're nothing like Susan. For one, you're quiet when you're upset."

She nodded. That was true. Beth liked even-keeled.

"I saw a picture of her, and Ellen thinks I resemble her."

Nick blew out his breath. Nice. What woman wanted to be told something like that? "Ellen's a little hard around the edges but soft once you get to know her."

Beth didn't look as if she believed him. "Do they still work?"

"They're both lawyers. Greg practices part-time, and Ellen retired after Susan died."

"I see." Beth closed her eyes and leaned her head back.

"Give them time. Right now they're afraid of you."

"Afraid of *me?*" She bolted upright and stared at him. "Why?"

Nick chuckled. "Because they don't know you yet."

He couldn't point out the obvious. His in-laws knew Corey was nuts about her. And now they knew he was, too. Beth wasn't a threat to their place in Corey's life but a welcome addition. Susan's parents would see that, too. Eventually.

"Where do you want to go for dinner?"

"Doesn't matter. You choose."

Great. This wasn't turning into the date he'd hoped for. Not with Beth practically hugging the passenger-side door as if she wanted to jump out. Obviously, a romantic dinner wasn't going to happen.

"We'll be okay, Beth. We're going to make this work."

She gave him a teasing smile, but it didn't cover the worry in her eyes. "I don't know. You come with a lot of baggage."

He chuckled again. "We both do, honey. We both do."

"Beth," a deep voice intruded.

She opened her eyes and stared into gray eyes that were awfully close to her own. "Yeah?"

"We're home."

She sat up and yawned. She'd fallen asleep after dinner, a very quiet dinner, while Nick drove home. "Sorry."

"Don't be. You're pretty when you sleep."

Beth laughed. "Yeah, right. Did I snore?"

"No."

"Good."

Silence settled heavy in the car.

Would Nick kiss her good-night? Should she let him?

After meeting Corey's grandparents, there were

other things to consider before moving forward. Her mom had said to follow her heart, but how could she when it was silent? Too many other variables to consider with a relationship with Nick. Namely what might happen to Corey if Nick died. If she was only a stepmom, would that mean anything in a court of law?

"Thanks for going with me tonight."

"You're welcome. I'm glad I went." Her eyes had been opened wider.

Nick leaned toward her. "I guess we should say good-night, then."

Beth didn't want to get out of the car. She didn't want Nick to leave, either. "Can you do me a favor?"

"Sure."

"Will you call me when you're done with your shift tomorrow?"

Nick smiled. "At seven on a Sunday morning?"

Beth nodded.

"You got it." He softly ran his finger down her cheek. "Maybe we can do dinner next week. Someplace nice."

"Not good. That's the last full week of school and a final push for Corey." She didn't ask for a rain check.

He narrowed his gaze. "You're not still considering holding him back?"

"No. Honestly, that wouldn't be good for him

now. Not when there's been so much improvement. But he's still not near a third-grade reading level."

Nick looked at her with hope in his eyes. "You could work with him over the summer."

Beth hesitated. "We'll see."

Nick sighed. "We'll talk more next week, then. While we're sailing."

"Yes."

"Beth..." Nick stopped and then leaned back in his seat. "Good night."

She tamped down her disappointment. He wasn't going to kiss her. A good thing, too, considering Beth's state of mind. The only whispers she heard from her heart told her to get out now before she got in too deep and drowned.

"Good night, Nick."

Chapter Thirteen

Beth held Corey's hand as they walked down the dock toward Gerry's boat. Nick held his son's other hand. She loved the strength that had developed between father and son. They were fine. They'd be fine, too. She'd done her job helping Corey read. And that was a good thing, even if it hurt to think about them without her.

Today she'd pretend they were any ordinary couple. She wouldn't ruin the day thinking about the what-ifs and what-she-should-dos. She'd simply enjoy her last outing with the Grey men and call it good.

"Wow. Is that it?" Corey pulled against Nick's other hand.

But Nick didn't let go. "Stay with me, bud."

Gerry's beautiful white sailboat rocked gently against a wave left behind by a motorboat. Beth nodded. "That's it."

Nick gave her a sharp look. "The *Showoff?* Does this guy have something to prove?"

Beth shook her head. "No, no. He's fine, really. Julie has always called Gerry a show-off, so when they got the boat, it was a natural choice for a name."

Nick looked skeptical.

Beth scanned the marina that was already bustling with activity. Boaters headed for town and breakfast and others prepped their sailboats and motorboats for a day on Lake Michigan. And what a day it promised to be. Not a cloud in the sky and temperatures climbing but with a steady breeze.

Perfect for sailing. Perfect for hitting the beach on South Manitou Island. And perfect for falling in love.... Wait, she'd already done that against her better judgment.

She glanced at Nick. Of all the guys she'd ever wanted, why'd she have to fall for this one? Nick had the potential to break her heart forever. And if anything happened to Nick, she might lose Corey, too.

That was a double whammy she didn't want to risk taking. Better to get out now. But after today. She wanted to enjoy today. She wasn't supposed to think about those nasty what-ifs.

"Morning!" Julie popped up out of the sailboat's cabin. "Have you guys had breakfast? We've got leftover fruit salad and sweet rolls."

"Thanks, but we ate at my mom's." Beth let go of Corey's hand and stepped down into the boat. She faced Nick when he didn't follow, shielding her eyes from the sun.

Standing on the dock holding on to a seven-year-old who strained to climb aboard, Nick hesitated.

"You coming aboard?"

"I'm not much of a boating guy, but I thought... I don't know what I thought."

Julie grinned. "You expected a big motorboat, didn't you?"

Nick nodded and finally let go of Corey, who jumped in with a whoop of delight.

"Can I go up there?" Corey pointed toward the front.

"No!" Nick's voice was sharp. Then he glanced at Julie and explained, "I don't want him falling over."

Julie opened one of the bench-seat compartments and pulled out a child-sized life vest. "One rule on our boat is that kids have to wear a life vest on deck. We've got enough for the adults, too. You boys okay with that?"

Corey nodded.

Nick looked as if he relaxed, a little. He helped his son into the life vest. Not one of those cheesy orange puffy ones but a Coast Guard–approved personal flotation device. Gerry had bragged about them last year after he'd upgraded his gear.

"A cool one," as Corey put it, making her heart pinch.

Beth ruffled the boy's hair.

"Coffee, anyone?" Julie offered. "We're waiting on Gerry's brother and his wife, and then we'll head out. They have a little girl around Corey's age. I imagine the kids will want to play in the berth."

"Berth?" Nick cocked his head.

"It's way up front in the cabin with a flat bed. The kids can play games and look out the windows. It's a good place for them while we're moving out. They can't fall out anywhere down there."

Nick nodded. "Then sure, I'll take a cup of coffee."

Beth declined. Once Julie slipped back into the cabin, she turned to Nick. "You sure you're okay with this?"

Nick gave her a tight smile. "Corey has been talking about nothing else all week. I can't chicken out now. You've done this before, right?"

Beth nodded. "Several times. Gerry's a good sailor. He grew up in Leland and has sailed Lake Michigan his whole life. He knows what he's doing."

Nick's gaze traveled the nearly thirty-foot sailboat while he ran his hand along the railing surrounding the back of the boat.

He finally blew out a breath. "Okay, then. Good. I'm good."

Beth chuckled and slipped into the cabin. She set the duffel bag she'd brought on a cushioned bench seat in the cabin's galley. She'd packed sweatshirts and windbreakers for the three of them, as well as beach towels and sunscreen. Nick had left his gun at home. Dressed for the beach, he couldn't exactly *conceal* it very well. Both Nick and Corey wore their swim shorts with T-shirts. Beth had her bathing suit on under her shorts and T-shirt.

Julie had informed her yesterday that the shoreline water temps were above normal for this time of year, so they might actually get in the water instead of wading around the beach.

Beth rolled her shoulders. She really needed this. A relaxing day spent in the sun with sand and surf.

It wasn't long before the other couple arrived. Their daughter, Millie, was a year older than Corey and in third grade.

"Millie, tell Corey about the tall-ship field trip." Beth wanted to stir Corey's interest and give him something to look forward to at school next year. Something more than how well he could read.

The little girl's eyes lit up. "Oh my gosh, it was so fun. We didn't go nearly as fast as Uncle Gerry, but we all got a turn to steer. It's a super-big boat with, like, these tall sails that make a lot of noise."

Corey listened with rapt attention.

True to Julie's words, the kids gladly followed her into the cabin toward the front. They seemed happy to stay put and play games until Uncle Gerry got the boat out into open water.

"Open water, huh? Like how open?" Nick sat beside her on the molded cushioned benches that made a horseshoe around the cabin entrance, surrounding the wheel.

Beth patted Nick's knee. "Don't worry. We're only fifteen miles or so from South Manitou Island and it's a straight shot. This is going to be fun."

He draped his arm around the ledge behind her. His fingers teased her neck along the collar of her T-shirt, sending shivers through her. "If you say so."

"I do." Beth forced a smile and then got up for a bottle of water.

She'd never have expected Nick to be nervous about sailing. He seemed so ready to face whatever came his way, but this was different. Maybe because he had to trust someone else's expertise for their safety. And maybe now he'd know a little about how she felt.

They made it. Nick climbed out of the inflatable dinghy with a small motor onto warm sand. They'd anchored in the crescent-shaped harbor of South Manitou Island, and a prettier place he'd never been. He felt like a pirate coming ashore to paradise, where a pristine sandy beach awaited them. He'd never seen water so blue.

He offered Beth his hand. "Watch your step."

She took it but gave him a "yeah, right" expression as she hopped out and skipped up the beach to lay out a blanket. Beth looked right at home, too, already kissed by the sun. Tall and blonde and tanned, she lured Nick's gaze often.

But she seemed distant today. Almost too cheerful, as if trying to keep something that bothered her at bay.

"C'mere, Corey. More sunscreen." Beth sprayed down his boy, whose red hair flamed and freckles multiplied in the sunshine.

Nick's did, too, so he'd keep his shirt on for a while yet. No need showing off his scars, either.

"So what'd you think?" Gerry slapped him on the back after setting down the cooler while his wife stuck a huge beach umbrella in the sand and opened it.

"Great trip. Thanks for inviting us."

Nick had to admit after they'd pulled out of the harbor and set sail across the Manitou Passage, he'd started to enjoy it. The light wind and soft waves and warm sunshine coaxed his muscles to relax.

Nick had even allowed Corey to follow Gerry around the railings that encompassed the deck to the front of the boat. The bow, as it was called.

Corey had loved watching their vessel cut through the wide-open water.

His boy had been beside himself with excitement when they spotted a long freighter to the north. If Corey's interest in boating stuck, Nick might have to find a little boat for them to use on the lake across the street. He had a smidgen of Lake Leelanau lake rights.

Gerry gave him a wink. "Good, now what about Beth?"

"She's amazing." Nick had no trouble admitting that, too.

Beth turned and smiled, but it was a sad sort of smile.

He smiled back.

Gerry laughed and slapped his back again. "We'll watch your boy if you two want to take a walk."

Nick glanced at his son. Corey and Millie had plunked down near the shoreline with sand buckets and shovels in hand.

Gerry pointed toward the lighthouse tower peeping up over the tree line. "That way is a shipwreck you can see from shore. It's a pretty good hike along the shoreline, but Beth knows the trail through the woods."

"Corey's going to want to see that."

"We'll meet you over there in a bit. Go on. It's quite a sight."

"Thanks."

Gerry nodded. "No problem."

Nick walked over to Beth sitting on the beach blanket. Sunlight shimmered in her hair. He sighed and offered his hand. "Let's take a walk."

Beth's eyes widened. "What about Corey?"

"They'll watch him and then meet us by the shipwreck. Gerry said you knew the way."

Beth took his hand and stood. "I do."

Nick needed to talk with Beth alone. "Corey, we're going for a walk. Mind Julie and Gerry, okay, bud?"

"Okay." His son continued piling sand.

He glanced at Beth. "He's good." Nick wasn't so sure about himself, though. Walking along the gorgeous stretch of shoreline in silence, he ran the question through his mind. Over and over, he came up with the same plan, and the same reasoning. But he couldn't nail down the answer.

"You're awfully quiet." Beth gave his hand a squeeze.

"Yeah." He glanced at her and his stomach dropped. He hadn't been this nervous in a long time. He stopped walking and reached for Beth's other hand. "I can say the same about you, too. What's going on, Beth?"

Her eyes widened but she didn't pull away. She didn't say anything either, but shrugged.

"Talk to me."

Her blue eyes clouded over. Guarded. "About Corey?"

"And us."

"I don't think we should do this now." She tried to pull her hands away, but he held firm.

"Why?"

She looked around. "It's too beautiful a day—"

That came like a kick in the gut. He'd hoped for so much more. "Would you consider watching Corey through the summer?"

Her eyebrows went up. "As his tutor?"

"No. Although, I sure could use your help with his reading."

Beth tipped her head. "You mean like in the mornings until my mother gets home?"

He pulled her closer and wrapped his arms loosely around her waist. "I mean to complete our family. For real. For good."

"Nick…" she warned.

He knew what he wanted. It hadn't taken long to know Beth was the woman he wanted to share his life with. Tired of dancing around the obvious, he dove straight in. "Marry me."

Her eyes went wide and softened and then watered.

"I can't." Her voice was whisper-low and full of regret.

"Why?"

She pushed out of his arms. "You know why."

"Because you won't date a cop? Come on, Beth. Don't you think we're past that?"

"It's bad enough worrying about you now. But if we— No. I can't go through that for the rest of my life. I won't."

"We're already a stable family for Corey. Doesn't that count for anything?" He threw his arms wide. "Look at this sailing trip. You recognize Corey's interests and feed them. You inspire him to succeed."

"So, you—"

He cut her off. "So, he needs both of us. He needs you as much as he needs me."

She closed her eyes and a single tear tripped over her lashes to run down her cheek.

He didn't want to make her cry and felt like a heel for doing so. Gently, he wiped the tear away as he tucked her hair behind her ear.

"He wants you for a mom," he said softly.

"That's not fair." Her voice was barely above a whisper.

"Love's not fair, but isn't it worth exploring?"

Her eyes flew open.

"I love you, Beth."

"Stop! Just stop." She backed away as if scared to listen. "I'm not marrying you, Nick. There's too much for me to lose."

Nick understood her fears, but he didn't want their lives ruled by it. Or their relationship stunted as friendship or ended because of it. How could he make her see that they had the right stuff to make it?

"But isn't there far more to gain, even if our life together is shortened?"

Beth searched his solemn gray eyes. So dear, this man, but he didn't get it. Her mother said she never once regretted marrying Beth's father, but had her mom really moved on? She still grieved. Still tried to fill the void left from her father's death.

She sighed. "Can we discuss this later?"

"If you'll reconsider."

"No. I'm pretty solid on this." Beth didn't flinch or look away, emboldened now that she'd finally made a choice. Was it the right choice?

Nick nodded, defeated. "Then let's see this shipwreck. The rest of the group expects to meet us there."

"Okay." Beth felt sick for doing this to him.

She walked alongside Nick as they rounded the corner toward the lighthouse. They shuffled through the water's edge and up on shore. Not all the sand was as smooth as in the protected harbor. They both wore their beach sandals, so it didn't matter.

Without a word, they crunched through zebra mussel shells bleached white by the sun. The beauty was lost to her. She'd made the right decision. Her mind ran through all the reasons why they'd struggle. She mentally listed the risks. Deep down she knew they all made sense. Logical reasons to refuse him, but it still hurt.

"This place is incredible," Nick said softly.

Beth jumped at the chance to act normal. Even if it was only small talk about the area, it was something. Something to stop the noisy thoughts inside her head.

"Wait till you see the shipwreck. It's sort of eerie but really neat and stands right out of the water. This whole area is a diving preserve because of all the sunken ships. Gerry and Julie have dived here before."

"Really? I didn't know. Lake Superior, sure, everyone's heard that song."

Beth chuckled despite the heaviness in her heart. Who hadn't heard about the wreck of the *Edmund Fitzgerald*? "There's quite a seafaring history on Lake Michigan as well as Superior. Amazing how these lakes can turn deadly."

Nick's brow furrowed and his skin paled. "Ah, I didn't need to hear that."

Beth stopped walking and faced him. The noise was back in her brain. "That's how I feel, Nick. Every time you go to work."

He kicked a piece of driftwood. "I know it's not easy. My parents may have split up because my mom couldn't handle the demands of my dad's job. But you're strong, Beth. More so than you realize."

She hadn't planned on doing this today. She'd wanted to discuss it later, but the words seemed to bubble up and flow out of her before she could stop them. "I don't know if I can handle it. If I can handle *us*. You can't promise to come home unharmed."

Nick looked at her. His eyes looked red-rimmed and lost. His nose was sunburned and his hair shone like burnished copper in the sun. He tipped his head back to look at the sky and then zeroed in on her. "Can anyone make that promise? Beth, we're in God's hands. Not our own."

Looking into Nick's somber eyes, she couldn't say another word. What argument did she have for that one? Other than her lack of trust in God to see her through the heartache of losing Nick. And that's what it all boiled down to. A matter of trust in the unseen and unknowable future. A strong person might be able to do that. But she wasn't strong. Not at all.

"What about Corey?" Nick asked.

Beth nodded. She fought against the pounding headache that echoed deep in her heart.

Corey needed stability and like it or not she was part of that stability for now. "I'll help through the summer as his tutor, but that's all I can be. It might be best for you to find another care provider."

Nick gave her that lopsided smile that wasn't much of a smile at all. "Corey's going to his grandparents' for a couple weeks. They'll keep up with Corey's reading and I'll look for someone else then."

Beth fought for control and managed a clipped nod. Her mother knew from the get-go that Nick would find someone else through the summer months, but this still felt like a betrayal. An end.

She couldn't hear any whispers from her heart now. Nothing came to her but a dull ache. She sighed. "Come on, let's see that wreck."

Nick looked at her with gloomy eyes, as though he'd lost his best friend. And maybe she had, too.

"I don't like the look of those clouds." Julie packed up what was left of dinner.

Nick overheard that muttered comment over the sound of the beach umbrella flapping furiously in the wind. Wind that had really picked up. He scanned the horizon, where those dark clouds Julie had mentioned hovered far away.

He'd hinted at leaving early a couple of times. It was pretty tough hanging out with Beth. Pretty tough to act normal when his heart had taken a beating. There was no getting her back from this one. No pushing for something more between them. Beth didn't want to be the wife of a cop. End of story.

"Wind's coming out of the west, southwest. I think we can outrun it." Gerry gave his wife a wide grin.

It was a braggart kind of grin that didn't give Nick much comfort. Great, this guy wanted to play cowboy.

They'd lingered too long over dinner, but Gerry wanted to wait and sail back by sunset. He said there was nothing like it. Well, Nick could have done without the added treat if it meant getting home safe and sound.

After an afternoon spent hiking and lounging on the beach, everyone was beat. But Gerry suddenly kicked into high gear. He and Julie moved quickly, getting their beach gear loaded onto the dinghy while the rest of them trudged along.

Nick remembered that kind of adrenaline rush. The anticipation of a challenge ahead. He could feel it bouncing off Gerry like a rubber ball. Only Nick wasn't feeling up to a challenge today. And he had a bad feeling this day was about to get worse. Fast.

"Come on, everybody. Let's go." Gerry waved his arm, gesturing to load up.

Nick looked at his beautiful but cowardly Beth. She wanted to run away from what they had, thinking it'd be easier. For who? Her? But the reality of how right she was hit hard. As the daughter of an officer, Beth had seen what it was like to be mar-

ried to a cop. Her eyes were wide-open. Maybe
he was the naive one thinking that love and faith
were enough to keep them together. All he knew
was that he loved her. Blindly, deeply and forever.

And that's why he'd let her go.

Beth didn't seem the least bit concerned about
the clouds as she helped the kids climb into the
smaller boat they used to shuttle back to the
Showoff.

He thought about that wreck of the *Morazan*
freighter they'd seen offshore sticking straight up
out of the water. Gerry had explained that she'd run
aground in the fall of 1960. There were a whole
lot of shipwrecks littering this Manitou Passage.
Big ships.

Bigger than the *Showoff.*

Nick rubbed the back of his neck where the hairs
felt prickly. He grabbed the life vest on the bench
seat of the dinghy. "Corey. Put this on."

His son's eyes went wide at his sharp tone.

"Please," Nick said softly.

He glanced at Beth.

She'd quieted, too, at his barked order.

Millie's parents gusseted her up in a life vest,
too. And the girl's father kept staring toward the
west and those clouds that were building.

The ride from shore was quick, but a distant
rumble of thunder quieted the chatter as they
climbed aboard the sailboat.

Nick looked around the cockpit and then asked Beth, "Where's the adult vests?"

She patted the cushioned benches. "Under here."

"Let's get them on."

"Dude." Gerry slapped him on the back after securing the dinghy to the back of the boat. "We're fine. We'll stay ahead of it. Might even miss it entirely, according to radar."

Nick reached under the bench anyway. "I'm used to wearing a different kind of life vest at work, so I'd feel better with one on."

"Suit yourself." Gerry ducked into the cabin.

"Beth?" He handed her one.

She narrowed her gaze and then slipped it over her T-shirt and secured it. She gave him a quick nod. Better to be safe.

The air hadn't cooled in spite of the stiffer wind. Warm southwest wind, Gerry had said. Nick didn't care where it came from. All he knew was that the chop on the water had increased by the time they had pulled out from the protection of the island's harbor into the open waters of the Manitou Passage.

Nick tried to remain calm, but forty-five minutes later the sun had been swallowed whole by those clouds. The ones Julie didn't like.

Nick didn't like them, either.

Those clouds had made a dark bluish-gray wall. The wall was gaining on them. Moving fast. He spotted a fork of lightning, but he kept his mouth shut. He didn't know how to sail; what orders could he possibly give?

Wouldn't have mattered if he'd spoken aloud—the wind would have stolen his words and thrown them away. He could barely hear himself think over the constant slapping of the wind against the sails and waves sloshing against the boat. Not to mention Gerry and his brother spouting out terms Nick had never heard.

They sort of tilted in the water. Nick held on tight and wedged himself in the corner where the cabin met the cockpit. When he spotted Gerry and his brother pulling on life vests, his stomach turned. They were in for a rough time ahead.

"Anything I can do?"

Gerry shook his head. "Go below for now with the women and children. It's going to get a little dicey and wet up here."

Nick swallowed a bruising retort.

"Wet and wild." Gerry's brother, on the right side deck, had a big grin on his face.

The two men enjoyed this a little too much. Nick understood the feelings from working undercover. Man against man, Nick knew his chances. Man against nature was something else entirely and completely unpredictable. He clenched his teeth as he slipped into the cabin. There were bigger reasons for this boat's name and he'd not spout them here and now. But he prayed those reasons wouldn't get them all into trouble.

In the cabin, Beth and Millie's mom sat tucked in by the little galley table. Julie had stashed things in cupboards and compartments that locked with a click before they left South Manitou. But she kept finding things that might dislodge and fly across the cabin, like the card game the kids played earlier.

Right now those two kids stared wild-eyed out the little cabin windows while they huddled on that flat surface in the front.

Julie and Millie's mom wore their life vests, too.

"This is so cool." Corey watched the waves that were too close to the left side window for Nick's comfort.

He didn't care for the spray of water that occasionally came into the cabin, either. "Yeah, cool."

Nick looked at Beth. She'd slipped on her windbreaker over her vest but still looked pretty calm. Maybe there was nothing to worry about. He was a novice at this kind of thing.

But when he sat down next to her and took her hand in his, she held on tighter than a death grip.

They were moving so fast. And the sound of distant thunder grew louder.

Closer.

Beth rethreaded her fingers through Nick's, glad

for his steely calm. If she held on tight enough, maybe some of that strength would seep into her, too. The rocking motion wasn't treating her well. All of them looked as if dinner wasn't getting along well with the waves. Except for Corey. The rough seas didn't seem to bother the kid at all.

They kept the cabin door open for air. Spray from the waves spattered through. Occasionally water whooshed right over the side into the cockpit, soaking Gerry at the wheel. The cold water spit against her bare legs and she wished she'd thought to bring pants.

The wind had considerably increased. She thought she heard twenty-five knots, maybe even thirty, bandied about by the guys above. The boat heeled far to the side when hit by a sudden gust and Gerry yelled directions to his brother.

Millie squealed and her mom reached for her.

Beth had slipped from her seat, but Nick caught her and pulled her against him. He looked a little green, too.

"You kids okay?" he called out.

Corey's eyes were huge as he lay on the bed in the V-shaped front of the boat. "What was that?"

"Hang on, bud." Nick's arms stayed locked around her.

Julie shrugged. "A hard gust of wind. We might have to go topside or we'll all be sick down here."

Beth glanced at the kids and shuddered. She felt

safer in the cabin, where the water couldn't pull them off the boat.

"Why can't we use the engine to motor us home?" Nick asked.

"The engine is for calm days and maneuvering around a harbor or close to shore. Totally ineffective in wind like this. It's okay—the storm will pass."

Beth took a deep breath. Hunker down and wait it out. They were safe in the cabin and dry. Julie and her husband had sailed in storms before. They'd ride this one out.

She closed her eyes and let her head fall onto Nick's shoulder. Helpless. She prayed they'd make it to shore soon, before she got sick. It'd been a long time since they'd left South Manitou. They had to be halfway across to Leland's harbor by now.

The wind only increased, taunting them, laughing at the men's attempts to harness it with sailcloth. Why had they done this, anyway? The sound of the wind was nothing compared to the roar of the rain. At first big drops hit the cabin roof with a *tap, tap, tap.* Then a deluge shrieked over the lake.

The boat heeled again, tipping farther this time. The kids screamed and even Julie looked concerned when a wave of water sloshed over the side of the stern into the cockpit.

"I'm going to get sick, Mama." Millie started to cry.

Nick got up but had to hold on to the table to keep from falling back down. "I can't stay in here."

Beth watched him make his wobbly way out of the cabin, but he leaned in the corner of the cockpit, hanging on to the railing. The rain, the waves and the lake were one color. Gray. She could barely see where the edge of the white boat stopped and the lake started, it rained so hard.

No way was she going out there.

"Yeah, we should all go up top." Julie tried to get up but slipped backward when the boat pitched again.

"No," Beth whispered. She wouldn't leave the cabin. "Corey, come sit by me, bud."

The boy scooted close and Beth held him tight.

"What's that?" Nick shouted.

"That's the crib!" Gerry yelled above the roaring rain. "It was portside a moment ago. Come about!"

"I can't see a thing," his brother screamed back. "Gerry!"

"Come about now!"

More howling wind and roaring rain.

The boat heeled hard. Beth came off her seat and fell on the floor, taking Corey with her.

"Get to the high side!" Julie pulled herself along the table.

Beth tried to get up but spotted the windows along the low side of the boat. They were covered by water. Her stomach dropped and then it felt as if they'd been lifted and tossed. She felt a shuddering crunch that made her teeth chatter.

"What was that?" Millie's mom whispered.

Turning her head, Beth saw that the young woman was on the floor, too. Millie had thrown up.

Beth's stomach lurched, but the bile inching up her throat froze. She trembled, closed her eyes and prayed her belly would settle when she realized what they'd hit.

How could Gerry not have seen the North Manitou Shoal Lighthouse smack in the middle of the passage? They'd passed it on the way, but its red light had been doused then, not needed. But what about a few moments ago?

An alarm rang.

"What's that?"

"Bilge alarm." Julie's eyes were huge, her face white.

"Julie, get everyone up here. We hit the corner of the shoal light. I don't know how bad it is."

Millie cried harder.

"How do we check it out?" Nick's deep voice echoed.

She opened her eyes in time to see Julie feeling along the cabin floor.

"What?" Beth cried.

Julie wobbled to the cockpit. "Gerry! We're taking on water into the cabin!"

"Grab the helm!" Gerry slipped around the

corner to the cabin desk devoted to charts and the radio. "Everyone out now! Nick, tether them in the stern for now. Julie will help you."

Beth watched as Nick sprung into action, helping Millie and her mom first out into the cockpit. Rain pelted them, pasting their hair against their heads as it soaked them through.

She glanced at the floor. Her feet were tucked up underneath her, and she was dry. Corey, too, because he sat in her lap. Where was the water coming in? Why did they have to go up top?

She couldn't move. Gripping Corey close, she tried to breathe evenly and think. Think!

"Mayday, Mayday, this is the *Showoff,* over." Gerry's voice sounded strained now.

She watched him as if she'd fallen into a bad dream.

The radio crackled to life and someone answered.

"We hit the crib and we're taking on water. Six adults and two children on board."

Beth listened as Gerry gave them their location, as well as their water situation. Something about pumps not keeping up but they had time.

They were taking on water! How much time did they have before they sank?

They were going to sink!

Beth couldn't hear the rest of what was said, because Gerry's voice had grown fuzzy.

They were going to sink.

"Nick!" she choked out.

"Come on, Beth. You and Corey. Now!" Nick shouted again. "Beth!"

She looked at him. He was tethered on to the railing and held out another tether. How would they unclip in time before they sank?

The wind still whipped. The boat sort of wallowed in the water but it wasn't going down. Gerry had adjusted the sails that now flapped in the wind. She glanced at the floor. Still pretty dry except for the darkening of the carpet toward the front end of the boat. Maybe they'd be okay. At least they weren't flying sideways anymore.

Corey clung to her.

She took a deep breath and stood.

Lord, please help us.

Gerry grabbed her arm. "Come on, Beth. It's okay. Help's on the way. The Coast Guard's already in the area somewhere. We're not the only one in trouble today. Once the storm passes, we'll abandon onto the dinghy. We'll be okay."

She looked at him and then at Nick.

"Come on, honey." Nick's smile was sweet.

She stepped out of the cabin, still clutching Corey, who walked beside her. Rain assaulted their faces. "Take care of him first."

Beth held on to Corey while Nick tethered in his son.

Another gust hit and the boat tilted.

Beth slipped and fell against the bench seat. Clawing against the cushioned seats, she couldn't grip the slippery vinyl. She slammed against the railing, flipped and went over.

"Beth!" Nick screamed.

She fought the waves, choked on them as they splashed over her face. The water was cold, but not as cold as the rain slicing her face.

She heard yelling and screaming. "Man overboard!"

Beth caught a glimpse of the sailboat. It rocked back and forth in the water. With all her might, she kicked and moved forward to the boat. The dinghy bounced on the waves behind it.

If she could reach the dinghy, she could pull herself in. She kicked with all her might and tried to swim forward but was tugged farther away by the waves.

Away from the sailboat.

Nick threw the life ring her way. "Grab it."

She tried. Felt the rope slip through her fingers and come up short as she was pulled away.

"Beth. Hang on."

"I'm trying."

Again with the life ring. But it didn't reach her this time.

Beth swam forward. The water dragged her back.

This time Nick threw something else her way. It hit the water and floated, tossed by the waves.

"Grab the seat cushion." Nick's voice barely skipped across the water's surface.

She swam toward the cushion, still out of reach. Sputtering after another wave swamped her. She tried again and managed to grip the canvas loop. Pulling herself onto the small square cushion, Beth rested, exhausted.

She watched as Gerry and his brother struggled to raise the sails, only to drop them back down. Everyone hunkered in the cockpit, hanging on. Gerry fought the waves but pulled the dinghy close to the stern. The *Showoff* didn't look as if it was sinking, but it rode lower in the water. Or was that the waves?

She saw someone pointing her way. Nick.

"I'm coming!" he screamed.

"No!" Beth reached out her hand. He couldn't leave Corey alone.

The boat waffled. Maybe they couldn't maneuver. She saw Julie let go of the rope to the dinghy. They couldn't come get her in that!

No. The dinghy wasn't going anywhere. And the waves pulled her farther away. She was on her own. Alone.

Chapter Fourteen

"Dad, no!" Corey clung to him.

Nick cupped his son's cheek. "I'll be back. It's okay, Corey. They've got you. You're safe until help gets here."

Nick scanned the horizon. No Coast Guard in sight. But then, Search and Rescue could come by boat out of Frankfort or by air in Traverse City. Didn't matter. Help was on the way.

His boy wouldn't let go.

"I'll get Beth and come back. I promise." Nick added that last bit praying God would make it so.

Beth was a strong woman and a swimmer to boot. He'd seen the lithe muscles in her arms and legs. If anyone could tread water for days, it'd be her. Only they didn't have days; they had hours. How many, he wasn't sure. Exposure to the warming but still-cold water temperatures worried him.

"Noooo." His boy sobbed.

Nick's gut twisted.

He was leaving his son behind again, but he couldn't leave Beth out there all alone. The seas were still too rough to take the dinghy and risk the kids' safety.

No, he had to go. Beth would have a better chance staying warm with both of them huddled close.

The storm was already blowing itself out, leaving so much damage in its wake. The *Showoff* was broken, but it wouldn't completely sink, according to Gerry. Too much flotation, he'd said. Whatever that meant. In Nick's mind, any boat could sink, including this one.

He glanced at the two men hanging on to the railing at the back, exhausted from their fight against the wind. The front end of the *Showoff* dipped below the water but then bobbed back up.

Smaller swells churned the dinghy against the sailboat, but their tie held firm. Julie had instructions to unclip the dinghy loose if the sailboat sank any farther.

Julie gripped Corey close. They both huddled with Millie and her mom. All of them shivering. But safe. His boy was safe.

Beth wasn't.

Nick could barely see Beth bobbing farther away from them, struggling to swim. "Corey, I have to go after Beth. We can't leave her out there all alone, can we?"

"No." His son hiccuped on a sob.

Nick pulled away, but Corey screamed. "Dad!"

"It'll be okay." He looked at Julie, who pulled his boy back away from the edge of the dinghy. "Don't let go of him."

"I won't."

"I'll be back, bud. I promise. I love you, son. I love you very much."

His son cried harder.

Nick looped a life ring over his shoulder and slipped into the water. His breath caught. It wasn't polar-bear-dipping cold, but certainly not shoreline warm like the harbor at South Manitou.

With the Coast Guard on its way and Gerry's boat equipped with a satellite tracking system, they'd be found. Hopefully soon.

But he had to get to Beth.

Nick swam hard and choppy. The waves pushed him forward. Toward Beth instead of away from her. God was with him. He knew that, but his legs tingled in the cold water. His fingers did, too. How long before they got into real trouble out here?

"Help me, Lord."

She was so tired.

And cold.

Pushing herself up on the seat cushion Nick had

thrown her, Beth tried to paddle, but her arms felt as if they'd fallen off. She couldn't feel her fingers anymore. She couldn't feel anything...but regret.

Regret stung sharper than the cold water twisting the skin on her toes and numbing her fingertips. Why had she gone sailing, why had she brought Nick and Corey along, and even more troubling, why was she so afraid to make them a real family with a marriage license?

She'd always lived a safe life. Through high school, college and even now Beth weighed the risks of every decision she made, choosing the easy way. The safe way. She'd always prided herself on being practical. But she was practically scared of her own shadow, if the truth be told.

She spotted the boat as it bobbed up on a swell. Then it disappeared. So far away.

Glancing to the west, where the leftover clouds had turned dark peach from the late-day sun pushing its way down behind them, Beth wondered if this might be her last sunset.

She closed her eyes. "Lord, I'm so sorry...."

What was she sorry for?

"Everything. Not trusting You. Not telling Nick and Corey how much I love them."

Nick...

Beth started to cry.

Nick had said they were all in God's hands. But Beth didn't want to believe it, not really. She'd been too wrapped up in keeping her heart safe from hurt.

God hadn't given her what she wanted; He'd given her what she needed. Who Beth needed in order to rely more on Him. Nick and Corey were gifts she'd refused.

How selfish could she be? Hurt was part of life, right? God never promised a carefree life without suffering. Yet she'd been striving for exactly that. Why rob them all of the blessing of being together because she was afraid of pain?

The fear of loss.

Beth never regretted a moment spent with her dad, even though his time with her had been cut short. Her father had taught her the importance of passion and love. But she'd traded those in for fear. She didn't want to face the possibility of Nick's death, and yet here she was facing her own.

She was going to die in this cold water.

And she'd never told Nick that she loved him.

A sob welled up and spilled over. Water splashed against her face as a wave lapped over her shoulders. She coughed and slipped back into the water. The seat cushion popped forward. Out of reach.

She didn't care.

Death is never final.

Was that her mom speaking?

Life is eternal.

Love never fades....

Beth let her head fall forward. Her face dipped into the water, startling her. Her hair had soaked up the cold water like a sponge and lay like stringy icicles against her neck. Her nose seared icy cold. With eyes closed, she smiled. At least, she thought she smiled; she couldn't feel her cheeks anymore.

God was with her. She felt Him drawing near. Lifting her up out of the water and breathing warmth on her face.

"I'm ready, Lord."

"Beth?"

Nick?

"Beth, honey. Come on, baby, talk to me." He swatted her face.

"Owww."

He laughed and then kissed her.

Heat.

Beth grabbed his hair and pulled.

"Owww."

"You're real." Beth's teeth chattered.

He chuckled. "Of course I'm real."

"Corey?"

"He's safe with the others. Help's on its way."

"Thank You, Lord." Her head flopped against Nick's shoulder encased in the life vest. He wore one at work, too. He was a careful man. Why hadn't she realized that before?

She kicked her legs, tried to stave off that tingling sensation.

"Come on, Beth. Fold your arms close to your body and keep still." He wrapped his arms and legs around her, pulling her close.

"Hmm, this is nice." She felt his body's heat seep into hers as they huddled together. Bobbing like human buoys.

He kissed her again.

Too brief.

She searched his storm-gray eyes, feeling stronger now. Now that he was with her. She slipped down and water splashed over her face again. She coughed and closed her eyes.

Nick lifted her higher, onto the life ring, and then held on to them both. "Stay with me. Don't sleep. We're going to be fine. And you're not leaving me. I'll get a desk job or something, anything to keep you with me. Is that understood?"

"No." She shook her head.

"What do you mean, no? No? I said you're not leaving me."

She smiled at how fierce he sounded.

Beth couldn't let him give up his passion because of her fear. She was done trading on fears and worries. "I love you, Nick. I love that you're a good father, a wonderful man and a careful cop."

He hugged her closer, if that was possible considering their life vests made a barrier between them. "Then marry me. You, me and Corey. Make us a family and we'll figure out the rest."

"Don't forget Peanut."

He rubbed his nose against hers. His was cold, too. "And the puppies, too. I love you, Beth."

"I'm glad." Her eyes itched and her lids lagged too heavy to keep open.

Her mom was right. God had whispered through her heart when she'd finally stopped and listened. Once the noise of her thoughts clamoring inside her practical, reasoning mind quieted. Out here in the water, she couldn't do anything but listen to the whispers in her heart. Did she really need to flip overboard for that? Why couldn't she have lain down on a bed of soft grass to hear…?

"Beth." Nick shook her.

She startled awake.

Nick held her close. "Kiss me."

She tried. She was so tired she could barely rally the strength to kiss him, but she managed. This was where she wanted to be and where she belonged.

Beth didn't know how long they huddled together in the middle of the Manitou Passage. When the sun finally dropped beneath the line of the lake's water, a Coast Guard rescue boat drew near.

Noisy, too.

Men shouted orders and their boat engine purred as it idled.

She shook her head. "Small boat."

Beth couldn't see the faces of the men leaning

down to get them up and out of the water because of the glare of lights that shone from behind them.

Nick laughed. "It'll do."

As they were pulled into the boat, Corey lunged for his father.

"Dad!"

Nick pulled him close and squeezed him tight.

Beth glanced at everyone huddled in blankets, but she couldn't raise a hand to wave. She was ushered into the cramped cabin before she could say another word. But then her teeth chattered something fierce and her eyelids grew heavy again. Someone helped her out of her windbreaker, life vest and clothes. Right down to her bathing suit.

And then a warm blanket was wrapped around her with packs of something warm placed directly on her skin. Her vitals were taken, including her temperature.

The heat washed over her like a warm wave followed by sharp needle pricks of tingling. Her feet went into warm slippers, and a warm hat with long woolly flaps was wound around her neck and head. Someone gave her a cup of hot chocolate, but her hand shook.

"Drink slowly." Someone held it for her.

Beth took a couple sips and then leaned back against the wall. Her head felt heavy.

"Is she okay?" Nick stripped off his wet T-shirt on his own.

Beth spotted a small, round puckered scar on Nick's shoulder with a bigger one on his back before the same kind of blanket went around him, too. A bullet wound. She'd touch that scar and make sure it didn't taunt her.

"Groggy, but good vitals. You're both hypothermic." The Coast Guard guy pointed at her. "She's borderline moderate, but I think she's warming well. Keep her still and we'll check her vitals again soon."

Nick nodded and sat down next to her. He scooped up Corey, also bundled in a blanket, onto his lap. Both were given hot chocolate.

"You okay?"

"Not the way I envisioned our sailing trip." Beth gave him a watery smile. "I'm so sorry."

He caressed her cheek before helping her take another sip of hot chocolate. "I'm not."

Corey looked up at his father. "I'm never going on a boat again."

Beth reached out her hand and patted the boy's knee. "Sometimes bad things happen, like today, but we can't let it make us afraid of living." She thought about Nick's scars. He might receive more over the course of his career, and she'd have to deal with that. Trust God to help her through the fear. "Or enjoying the beauty around us and trying again."

Corey's eyes went wide and he looked up at Nick.

"She's right, son. But we'll take it easy for a while. Maybe stick to Lake Leelanau."

Corey looked as if he thought hard about that one.

Beth smiled at the boy. "There's a great beach by your house."

"Soon to be our house." Nick took hold of her hand and kissed it.

Beth smiled. "Yes, soon to be our house. Nick, I don't want you to change what you do. Not for me."

"Beth—"

She cut him off with her fingers against his lips. They'd handle this together with openness and honesty. She was a cop's daughter who could teach Corey a thing or two about being the child of a deputy officer. She'd trust God to help her be a good cop's wife. One who'd give her fear and worry to God. He could handle it. She couldn't on her own.

"Bad things happen, but we're not going to live in fear. God is with us and we're in His hands. Right, Corey?" Nick echoed her words, but his gaze remained locked on hers.

Corey poked his dad in the ribs. "Is Miss Ryken going to be my new mom?"

"Is that okay with you?"

Corey nodded, but he wore a serious look on his face.

"What is it, bud?" Nick asked.

Beth held her breath.

"I'm glad because we're already a family."

"Yeah, bud. We are." Nick gave her that lopsided grin that wasn't much of a grin.

It made her heart ooze. Completely thawed out and pliable.

"Dad?"

"Yes, son?"

"Do I have to still call her Miss Ryken?"

Beth laughed.

Nick did, too. "I think it'll be okay if you call her Beth."

"I love you. I love you both." She leaned forward and hugged these two men brought into her life so that she might truly live.

They were a family. And they would remain a family no matter what.

Nick wrapped his arms around her. They had Corey trapped between them, but he snuggled in close.

This was real warmth. Real peace. And Beth was never so grateful for God's whispers into her heart in the dark waters of Lake Michigan. He had been with her then and she needn't fear the future, because He'd always be with her. With all of them.

Epilogue

The first Saturday in August shone like a gem-stone. A perfect summer day that remained warm and calm into early evening. It was the perfect day for Beth and Nick to exchange their wedding vows aboard a passenger ferry boat while cruising the Manitou Passage shoreline.

Beth had come up with this plan for a couple of reasons. She wanted to face the waters where they could have lost each other with a new memory of celebration. She also wanted to show Corey that they didn't need to live in fear of what had happened. God had been with them, and Beth wanted to honor that by marrying Nick where he'd proposed and she'd accepted.

Beth smiled as Corey led her down the aisle of the lower deck. The boy looked handsome in his khaki pants and crisp linen shirt that matched his father's. No suits and no ties. That had been the only request from her Grey men.

The lower deck's windows were open to let in the warm evening air too still for even a breeze. But that was okay with Beth. She'd take balmy to breezy on this special day.

The sides of the benches had been decorated with white bows and sprays of evergreens and wildflowers that she and her mother and Corey's grandmother had gathered earlier in the day in an open field near Nick's house.

Beth carried a small bouquet of the same.

"This is weird," Corey whispered. "Getting married on a boat."

"It's worth it, though, don't you think? Kinda fun, even?"

Corey shrugged. "I guess." Beth smiled down on the boy who'd stolen her heart the day he'd shown up in her class.

"Hey, Beth?" He looked up with a frown. "Do you think the puppies will be okay?"

"We'll take good care of them while you're with your grandparents." She squeezed Corey's hand and then smiled at Nick, who looked curious about their chitchat. She'd fill him in later.

Her mom had promised to stay with the dogs while they drove a couple hours north to spend a few days in a little cottage on Lake Michigan. The plan was for her mom to take two of the puppies by summer's end. And they'd keep Peanut and her other two. Much to Nick's chagrin, Beth didn't have the heart to send those puppies too far. And Corey had agreed.

They finally reached Nick standing tall and handsome with their minister and the boat's captain. Beth leaned down and kissed Corey's forehead when he handed her over to Nick.

"Thanks, Corey."

He gave her a serious nod and then sat down next to his grandparents.

"You look beautiful." Nick lifted her hand and kissed it.

"Thanks. You, too." Beth wore a simple white dress with her hair pinned up with more wildflowers. Even her strappy sandals were comfortable.

They had a long evening ahead of them. After the wedding followed by light hors d'oeuvres on the boat, dinner and dancing awaited at a restaurant overlooking the beach. Beth and Nick's guest list had been small. Family and a few friends.

The minister started the ceremony, and Beth stared into Nick's eyes and held tight his hands.

"To have and to hold in sickness and in health…'

Nick had held her in the water. He'd kept her warm and safe from slipping into a more serious situation. He helped her realize who to trust with her life and his. "I do."

Nick smiled at her.

"Nicholas, do you take Elizabeth to be your lawfully wedded wife…" the minister continued.

Beth experienced a renewed sense of pride in Nick's position. He enforced the law. Something not everyone could do. She'd support him in his calling. All things were possible in God, who'd strengthen her.

"I do."

"Then go ahead and kiss your bride."

Nick pulled her close. "I love you."

"I love you," Beth whispered before kissing Nick.

"Mr. and Mrs. Grey, folks," the minister announced.

Their guests cheered.

Beth spotted her mom, who dabbed her eyes with a tissue. And then she was practically tackled by Corey as he hugged them both.

She laughed and squeezed the boy closer. "I love you, Corey."

"Me, too." He buried his head into her waist.

He was her little boy now. For always.

* * * * *

Dear Reader,

Thank you so much for picking up a copy of my book. I hope you enjoyed reading Beth Ryken's journey to a happily-ever-after of her own. Beth was one of those secondary characters who demanded a book. At first I thought she and Eva's brother might get together, but no. They would never have worked!

And then I realized something about Beth. She needed to be needed but also played it much too safe because of the death of her police officer father when she was fourteen. Enter Nick Grey, a simple man called to be a cop. Both have emotional baggage, but when they finally place their trust in God and give Him their fears, their happily-ever-after is truly possible.

I love to hear from readers. Please visit my website at jennamindel.com or drop me a note c/o Love Inspired Books, 233 Broadway, Suite 1001, New York, NY 10279.

Many blessings to you,
Jenna

Questions for Discussion

1. When the book opens, Beth is worried about her mom's spending habits. Should she be? How could Beth have approached the issue more effectively?

2. Nick's relationship with his seven-year-old son is strained. What could Nick have done better to reach his boy?

3. Many youngsters struggle in first and second grade. Do you believe in having a child repeat those grades if they are behind grade-level standards? Why or why not?

4. Beth's and Nick's attraction to each other is immediate but they let their fears get in the way of deepening the relationship. Why were they afraid? How did they finally overcome those fears? And in what ways did their faith help?

5. Nick believes his previous mother-in-law feels threatened by his relationship with Beth. Should he have shared those thoughts with Beth? What steps can they take to keep Corey's maternal grandparents feeling connected?

6. Nick tries to overcome Beth's concerns regarding the possible dangers of his job by telling her that they are ultimately in God's hands. Do you believe that? If so, how can that put worry to rest in your life?

7. When their dog Peanut is in trouble with her labor, Nick calls his minister for prayer. How concerned do you believe God is about our pets? Have you ever prayed for yours? If so, what were the circumstances and how did God answer those prayers?

8. By the end of the book, Beth faces her biggest fear. Are there any fears you'd rather not deal with? And if so, how can you give them to God?

9. The Scripture verse of Isaiah 43:1–2 really spoke to me for this book. No matter how deep our troubles, God is with us and we won't "drown." What does this verse mean to you?

10. Heroes and heroines in romance novels often fall in love quickly. Do you think couples should date for a certain amount of time before marrying? If so, how much time is enough time? Why?

11. Beth agrees to tutor Corey and she uses a lot of games to teach. How essential is having fun to learning?

12. Do you remember your favorite book as a child? What was it?

LARGER-PRINT BOOKS!

GET 2 FREE
LARGER-PRINT NOVELS
PLUS 2 FREE
MYSTERY GIFTS

Love Inspired®

SUSPENSE
RIVETING INSPIRATIONAL ROMANCE

Larger-print novels are now available...